Dallas couldn't marry him

"How can we even consider marrying, the way we feel about each other?" she asked, shaking her head. "What kind of environment would that be for Nicky? Pretending to be husband and wife even if only for a few months."

Clay stood at the window, staring out. "Make no mistake about it—this would be no pretend or temporary marriage. We'd stay married as long as Nicky needed us." He turned. "How old are you?"

Her eyes widened in surprise. "Twenty-four."

"And I'm thirty-one. Too young to find the prospect of a celibate marriage acceptable."

"Surely you don't mean us? Me and you—?" She broke off, the growing darkness of his eyes warning her she was on dangerous ground. . . .

Jeanne Allan lived in Nebraska, where she was born and raised, until her marriage to a United States Air Force lieutenant. More than a dozen moves have taken them to Germany and ten different states. Between moves, Jeanne spent time as a volunteer. With her two teenage children, she enjoys nature walks, bird-watching and photography at the family's cabin in the Colorado mountains, and she enjoys all kinds of crafts, including making stained-glass windows. She has always liked to write, but says her husband had to bully her into writing her first romance novel.

Jeanne Allan was named Romance Writer of the Year for 1989 by the Rocky Mountain Fiction Writers.

Books by Jeanne Allan

HARLEQUIN ROMANCE

RANCHER'S BRIDE

Jeanne Allan

Harlequin Books

TORONTO • NEW YORK • LONDON
AMSTERDAM • PARIS • SYDNEY • HAMBURG
STOCKHOLM • ATHENS • TOKYO • MILAN

Original hardcover edition published in 1990
by Mills & Boon Limited

ISBN 0-373-03175-0

Harlequin Romance first edition February 1992

RANCHER'S BRIDE

CHAPTER ONE

'YOU'RE getting married?' Dallas blinked. Clay Dalton did not disappear. He was still sitting in her living-room as much at ease as if he had flown all the way to Alexandria, Virginia merely to have tea. 'I didn't know... Alanna never mentioned...'

'It was a sudden decision.'

'Why fly all the way out here to tell me?'

'Nicky.'

Dallas burrowed into her favourite chair, seeking comfort from the soft, silken cushions that enveloped her. Kicking off her shoes, she curled her legs beneath her, conscious of mud-splattered stockings and a chill that was caused by more than the weather. Clay lounged on the low sofa across from her, his long legs stretched out in front of him and crossed at the ankles. He was the image of a highly successful businessman in the well-tailored suit that clothed his tall, lean body. It was the stark contrast of tanned, leathery skin against a white shirt collar that betrayed his outdoor occupation. Squint lines radiated from blue eyes that were darker than the narrow stripes in his fashionable shirt.

She'd spotted him the minute she'd turned the corner and started up the slight incline towards her town house. Worry for Nicky had immediately leaped into her mind. 'You said Nicky was all right,' she reminded him now.

'She is. At the moment.'

Fear clutched at Dallas's heart, and then she realised what Clay was doing. 'Scare tactics won't force me to back down. I happen to believe that Nicky would be better off with me.'

'You think the judge would agree with you? A single woman,' he glanced at his watch, 'who works long hours and comes home looking as if making a cup of hot tea would be too much effort for her, much less cooking a healthy dinner and dealing with an active six-year-old. Look at yourself.'

'I know how I look. It happens to be raining out.' She'd forgotten an umbrella this morning, and her hair was plastered against her face from the chill February rain. Even her bones ached with exhaustion, but not because of the dreary day. The morning in court had done that. If she wasn't so depressed, she might find some irony in the situation. Dallas Wyatt coolly testifying in a custody case. Easy enough to remain cool when the participants weren't your own flesh and blood. Her gaze locked with Clay's. He was studying her, disapproval written on his face. 'Don't tell me you flew all the way from Colorado just to get my blessing.'

Clay straightened up, his eyes narrowing slightly at her sarcastic tone. 'No? You don't care who Nicky's future mother is going to be?'

Dallas gripped the arms of the chair. 'Alanna left Nicky to me. She said so in her will. I always promised her if anything happened to her...' She swallowed hard, unable to go on.

Clay ran his fingers through his dark brown hair. 'And Kyle named me in his will as guardian of his daughter if his wife predeceased him.'

'But you don't know that she did. Kyle might have died first. They were both dead by the time they were found.' She glared across the room at Clay. 'I intend to fight you in the courtroom, and I intend to win.'

'Damn it, Dallas, listen to me.' A muscle twitched in his clenched jaw. 'In Colorado a judge is not bound by the wishes of deceased parents. He'll take them under consideration, of course, but his primary goal is to protect the minor child, and he'll do whatever he finds to be in her best interest. And this particular judge's reputation is well known. He's dead set against single parents. I don't imagine that a single woman who arrives home after six o'clock at night is going to favourably impress him.'

'And you will? A bachelor?' Disconcerting titbits from Alanna's letters appeared in her mind with startling clarity: Clay's hedonistic style of living, his partying, his women.

Clay abruptly changed the subject. 'You know my mother died when I was ten.'

Dallas nodded. 'Alanna told me.' Clay's mother had been out riding alone and for some reason had dismounted and tied her horse to an old wooden fence. Apparently something had frightened the horse, a snake perhaps, and the horse had reared up, taking part of the fence with him. In his frenzy, he'd flung the attached board around, breaking his own leg and striking Mrs Dalton in the head, killing her instantly. Dallas felt sure that this latest tragedy had brought back to Clay his own sorrow when his mother had died. She felt her way hesitantly. 'You're admitting that Nicky needs a woman around.'

'Yesterday I went into the house before lunch and found her sitting on the stairs. She was sucking her thumb and simply staring off into space. The most pathetic, loneliest-looking child I've ever seen. That's when I decided.' He brushed off one knee of his trousers. 'To ask you to marry me.'

'Me? Marry you? You must be joking.'

'I couldn't be more serious.'

'Why me?'

'There isn't anyone else.'

The brutally honest reply stung. 'How romantic,' she mocked softly. 'Does this mean that you're not going down on bended knee?' Her hands curled into fists. Did he really think that she'd leap to do his bidding? 'The answer is no.'

Clay stood up. 'I can see that reasoning with you would be a waste of time.' His nostrils flared in anger. 'I don't know why I bothered to come, but I made the mistake of thinking that you care about Nicky.' He stalked down the hall and grabbed his coat.

'Clay, wait.' Dallas was on her feet. 'All right. I don't like you, but I love Nicky. For her sake, I'll listen.' When his face showed no signs of relenting, she said, 'Please. At least admit that your idea came as a shock.'

Clay tossed his coat on the floor. 'After the funeral, I swore I wouldn't speak to you again unless I was forced to in court.'

'What changed your mind?' She sank back into her chair. 'For heaven's sake, sit down and quit looming over me.'

Clay lowered his body into the chair across from her. 'Nicky. I'm almost positive that marrying anyone would give me the edge over you in court, but——'

'But you don't want to take that chance.'

'You love Nicky and she knows you. Anyone else would be a stranger. Maybe the wicked stepmother is a myth, but Nicky has suffered too much for me to gamble on her happiness.'

'Wicked stepmother...' The echoed words trailed off. Stunned by the unwelcome picture that Clay had painted, Dallas shook her head helplessly. 'I couldn't bear it if Nicky... it was hard enough when the judge gave you temporary custody so she wouldn't have to move right away. At least I knew you loved her. Surely you wouldn't marry someone who...'

'Marry me and the question doesn't arise,' Clay said impatiently. 'We can fly out to Las Vegas and get married and be home before the case comes to court.'

'But it's wrong. Dishonest.'

'What's dishonest about it? People get married for all kinds of reasons. Providing a home for Nicky, giving her a loving mother is as important as any of them. Nicole Dalton carries my brother's genes, my blood. I'll fight for her happiness in every way I can.' He looked at her, his eyes dark with suppressed emotion. 'And if that means marrying you, then, so help me, I'll do it. Whether you want to or not.'

'You can't force me.' Her voice came out a defiant squeak as Clay sprang from his chair.

'It was all just talk, wasn't it? You don't want Nicky.' He ignored her denial. 'If I married the first woman I met on the street she'd probably be a better mother to Nicky than you would. I knew you were tainted with the same blood as Alanna, but she, at least, cared for Nicky.'

'So do I! I love her! But my job, my...' She shrank back at the look of contempt on Clay's face.

'You just keep telling yourself how much you love her. And hope your dreams won't be disturbed by the cries of a little girl you abandoned because you were all talk and no heart.'

The panicky sensation of being swept headlong into a raging maelstrom flooded over her. She sensed that

Clay would be a relentless adversary. 'It's not fair,' she managed.

Clay was pacing the length of her living-room, and he turned at her protest. 'Fair? Is it fair that my mother died when I was only ten? Is it fair that Nicky's parents were killed in an automobile accident? Is it fair that I lost my only brother?' He smacked his fist against the back of her sofa. 'Is it fair that I'm forced to marry a woman I don't like simply to provide for my niece?'

His harsh words convinced her of the utter insanity of his plan. She couldn't marry him. Slowly she shook her head. 'How can we even consider marrying the way we feel about each other? What kind of environment would that be for Nicky? Two people who dislike each other living in the same house. Pretending to be man and wife, even for a few months...'

Clay stood at the window, staring out into the black night. 'Make no mistake about it. If you agree to my proposal, this would be no pretend or temporary marriage. We'd stay married as long as Nicky needs us.' He turned. 'How old are you?'

Her eyes opened wide in surprise. 'Twenty-five.'

'And I'm thirty-one. Too young to find the prospect of a celibate marriage agreeable.'

'Surely you don't mean...us? Me and you? I mean, there must be other women... I wouldn't expect you to give up——' She broke off, the growing darkness of his eyes warning her she was on dangerous ground.

'Are you proposing that I take a mistress?'

The contempt in his voice made her feel an awkward fifteen again. 'Yes—no—I don't care. It has nothing to do with me.'

Clay uttered a harsh laugh. 'You have an odd notion of marriage.'

'We're not getting married. Even if I did consider your ridiculous idea, a marriage of convenience...' She swallowed the rest of her sentence as Clay stood in front of her.

He pulled her from the chair. 'There would be nothing convenient about it,' he said, scowling at her as his fingers bit into the soft flesh of her upper arms. 'But, since you're so concerned about the proper environment for Nicky, ask yourself what kind of family life we would have if I spent all my evenings tomcatting around.'

Her skin burned beneath his touch. 'The whole idea of our getting married is ludicrous enough, without ... that.'

'Is it?' Clay encircled her waist and imprisoned her chin with his free hand. The glint of anger in his blue eyes hinted at emotions held under tight control.

A shiver of fear ran up her spine. His determination frightened her while his overwhelming masculinity engulfed her. Her body was too aware of his. She must not allow him to overpower her common sense. 'Two people who intensely dislike each other... I couldn't possibly consider sleeping with you.'

The arm at her waist tightened. 'No? I was thinking maybe *that* part of our marriage wouldn't be such a sacrifice.'

Her stomach plummeted to her knees at the sensual tone in his voice. 'It would be for me,' she managed to say.

Clay thrust his fingers into her hair, forcing her to lean back against his arm at her waist, a movement that pressed her hips against his. The awkward stance strained her neck as he studied her face, his fingers pressing deep into her scalp. 'Let's see about that, shall we?' he muttered against her lips, and then his mouth closed over hers. Dallas stiffened, but before she could draw away Clay set out on a voyage of gentle exploration, nibbling her lips with his teeth and tracing the contours of her mouth with his tongue.

Dallas knew Clay's kiss was a calculated move to impose his will upon her, but the heat which flooded her body from the intimate contact undermined her will to resist him. She slid her hands up his chest, her fingers curling around his neck. He increased the pressure on her mouth until her lips parted before his searching tongue. Their mingled breathing was harsh in the silent room, and Clay's masculine scent filled her nostrils. His hands roamed over her back, tracing her spine. Heat spread throughout her body, sending a fevered flush to the surfaces of her skin and collecting in a molten pool deep within her.

Clay lifted his lips from hers. 'Well.' He cleared his throat. 'Now that we've settled that, how soon can you be ready to move?'

Dallas tore herself from his embrace, furious with herself for succumbing to such a blatant seduction. If only she hadn't gratified Clay with her response. To hide her mortification, she lashed out at him. 'We didn't settle anything. The kiss changes nothing. Marriage between us is out of the question. You hated Alanna, and I can't forgive Kyle for making the last days of her life miserable. You look at me and see Alanna. And I...'

'Look at me and see Kyle.'

'No,' she half whispered. 'I look at you and see a man who closed his eyes to his brother's behaviour. Behaviour that was obviously a cry for help.'

Clay paled beneath his tan. 'And now you hate me so much that you're willing to sacrifice Kyle's daughter.'

'No! Let her live with me.'

'If you want her, you'll have to marry me. Yes or no?'

Dallas knew that she was as white as Clay. How could she answer when her mind was numb? 'I-I can't.' Tears built up in her throat and her mouth wobbled. Refusing to look at him, she slowly shook her head. 'I'm sorry.' She felt the instant chill as he moved away from her.

'I'm sorry, too. I shouldn't have come. Marrying me would mean a tremendous sacrifice on your part. You'd have to give up your job, your home, your friends—disrupt your entire life for someone else's child. It's too much to ask of a woman. Goodbye, Dallas.'

His footsteps rang loudly as he crossed the wooden floor in the hall, but not as loudly as the words he'd spoken rang in Dallas's ears. She stirred uneasily. What was she doing? Selfishly allowing her own private concerns to take precedence over the life and happiness of a child who'd never harmed a soul. Nicky. Sweet, innocent Nicky. How could she stand there and fault Clay for refusing to help his brother when she was refusing to help Nicky? 'All right,' she said. 'I'll marry you.'

Clay stopped, his hand on the door. 'Are you sure?' he asked over his shoulder.

'No.'

He gave a short laugh and turned. 'You're honest anyway. What made you change your mind?'

Fear of the drastic step she had just promised to take goaded her into an angry reply. 'Not your patronising male chauvinism. I'm capable of sacrificing just as much as you are, even if I am a woman.'

'I wasn't issuing a challenge.'

'Weren't you?' She waved off his answer. 'Never mind. It doesn't matter.' She drew a shaky breath. 'I need a drink. I cooked beef burgundy last week—there's some wine left.'

Glass in hand, Clay toasted her. 'To the blushing bride.'

Dallas's hand tightened around the stem of her glass. Cold reality struck her. She was actually going to marry this man—for real. Not in some cardboard facsimile of marriage. He expected her to join with him in a union of the most intimate kind. Would he expect to stay with her tonight? Courage fled. 'Clay, I——'

A rough finger pressed against her mouth. 'Don't back out now.'

'I wasn't. I——'

'Good.' Clay drained his glass and set it on the table. He pulled a small notebook from his pocket. 'I made some notes on the plane flying out here.'

'Were you so sure of me?'

'I was sure of your love for Nicky.'

A bitter suspicion took root in Dallas's mind. Clay had known all along which buttons were the right ones to push. He'd never intended to leave Virginia without her consent to his proposition. She dumped her wine in the sink and made herself a cup of instant coffee. It was crucial to establish from the very beginning that Clay was not always going to get things his way. 'There are a few conditions,' she announced. Her voice barely wobbled.

The plane's engines droned in her ears, the repetitive sound exacerbating nerves already worn raw by the events of the past week. One week, only seven days, but long enough to totally change the course of one's life. Last week she had been Dallas Anne Wyatt, spinster and elementary school counsellor. She looked down at her left hand—a gold band sparkled in the sunlight. This week she was Mrs Clayton Peter Dalton, wife and almost mother. Almost, because the court hearing wasn't until next week.

She glanced across the cockpit. That Clay could pilot a plane was only one of the many discoveries that she was making about her husband. He approached life with a self-assurance that sometimes bordered on arrogance and overrode obstacles with the confidence of a man to whom nothing was impossible. Her new husband liked a huge breakfast, hated television, cursed telephones and spent an inordinate amount of time on them. He was considerate to waitresses and salespeople but had no patience for incompetence or stupidity. He had to shave twice a day and ate his steaks rare.

He slept on the right side of the bed—a fact that she knew only from noticing which side of his bed was rumpled. He had moved into her town home to help her with the myriad details involved in quitting her job and moving, but they had not slept together—a condition that she had made. If custody of Nicky was not granted to them, there would be no impediment to their seeking an annulment. Clay had not even kissed her since the night they'd agreed to marry. Unless one counted the perfunctory peck on her cheek that had followed their hasty wedding in the small chapel in Las Vegas this morning. From the moment that Dallas had agreed to his proposal, Clay had been polite, considerate and perfectly willing to postpone intimacies. Of course, he'd already got his way about the marriage.

Dallas looked out of her window. The Colorado landscape mirrored her marriage. On her right, the snow-topped mountains were beautiful. And as cold and forbidding as her husband. Below them, the countryside sprawled, barren and inhospitable. Cars beetled along concrete ribbons, no doubt anxious to reach more civilised surroundings. The only other sign of life was the shadow of the small plane they'd boarded in Colorado Springs, the plane that was swiftly carrying her towards the Dalton Ranch. Towards an existence that bore little relationship to the one she'd left behind.

Dallas was swamped by a wave of longing for Alexandria. Today was Saturday. Back in Virginia she could be getting on the underground Metro headed towards Washington DC to see an exhibition at the Smithsonian Institution or to have tea at the Hay Adams Hotel or to browse through the Shops at National Place or Garfinckel's.

Garfinckel's. Where Clay had purchased, over her objections, the short, simple white dress she'd worn for their wedding. Wedding dresses celebrated unions of love. Dallas would have been content to wear the first dress she pulled from her wardrobe, but Clay had insisted, saying that she'd only get married once. A chilling reminder that there would be no turning back.

The hard knot in Dallas's stomach grew. This was her second trip to Clay's Colorado ranch. The first had been for the funeral. Her parents had been unable to get there from Germany. At the cemetery slashing pellets of snow had driven the tears from her face, but Kyle's family had been dry-eyed and stone-faced. It wasn't until afterwards that Dallas had discovered that they blamed Alanna for the fatal accident. In her hurt and bewilderment Dallas had lashed out at them. At least there was another Dalton son. Her angry defence of her cousin had hardly endeared her to them, and now she was planning to live among those very people.

'Not long now,' Clay said. 'Those two mountains ahead of us are called the Spanish Peaks. Indian legend has it that the rain gods live on the summits. The thin ridges of rock around the peaks are volcanic dikes. Just north of them is La Veta and the small airport we use.' He sounded more like a tour guide than a groom bringing his brand-new bride to her new home.

Nervously Dallas twisted the band on her finger.

The movement caught Clay's eye. 'Too tight?'

Suffocating, she wanted to shout. But she didn't. She had made her decision based on what was best for Nicky. It was too late to change her mind. Besides, she wasn't the only one entrapped in this loveless marriage. Not that Clay's situation could be compared to hers. He was returning to his home, his family, his friends. There was no reason for him to be terrified—as she was. She fought the panic that threatened. Clay was still waiting for his answer. 'No, it's fine.'

Clay frowned. 'So what's the matter?'

'This isn't exactly how I anticipated my wedding-day,' she evaded.

'Me neither.' He paused. 'I'm sorry your parents couldn't make it.'

'It's just as well. In spite of my explanations, Mother persisted in treating this as some type of Cinderella story. All she could talk about was how I followed you around at Alanna's wedding.'

Clay chuckled. 'You were so skinny. With a mouth full of braces.'

The amusement in his voice cut deep. It was painful to remember the gawky teenager who'd fallen head over heels in love with the groom's brother. The week of the wedding had been a gay whirlwind. When they weren't at parties, Dallas had dragged Clay on a sightseeing tour that had encompassed all the historical and cultural sights in the DC area. He'd seemed to share her enthusiasm for sitting in George Washington's church pew, or peeking into Robert E Lee's childhood bedroom, or listening to the recorded words of Abraham Lincoln, or wandering the halls of Congress. She'd thought that he was interested in her anecdotes of famous personalities and her favourite museums. It wasn't until Alanna had taken her aside after the wedding that Dallas had learned that Clay had been making fun of her and her youthful enthusiasm behind her back the entire time. Even now, ten years later, the knowledge still hurt. Pride required that she treat the subject lightly. 'You poor thing. Everyone knows it's required for the maid of honour to fall in love with the best man, but you must have been terribly embarrassed.'

'Actually, I was flattered. You were sweet and bubbly and you saw good in everyone. I can still remember that wide-eyed, innocent look on your face when you wanted me to kiss you. I was tempted, but I knew you were too young, that you'd never been kissed before.'

'I'd been kissed lots of times,' she lied. 'By boys. You were six years older. I wanted to know how a man kissed.'

Clay shifted in his seat. 'Alanna always boasted that she was your role model, that you were exactly like her. I never believed it could be true.' He stared out of the window. 'But you're a carbon copy of her, aren't you?'

'I'd be flattered if that were true,' Dallas said, 'but I own a mirror.'

Clay waved a dismissive hand. 'I don't mean in appearance. Alanna's hair was dark brown, almost black, her eyes were green and her skin milky white. She was dramatic, exotic, a hot-house orchid blooming in the desert. A person could be deceived into thinking that you were the farmer's daughter.' He reached over and touched the tip of her nose. 'No freckle would have dared mar Alanna's perfect nose. You've got almost as many as Nicky has.'

Dallas pushed away his hand, wounded by his disparaging appraisal. 'Alanna and I were only cousins.'

'Yet you seem to have a number of her habits. The same twist of your head, your walk, the way one corner of your mouth turns up when you're amused. Not that I've seen you amused very often.'

'My life hasn't been very amusing lately.'

'That's odd. Mine's been a real barrel of laughs.' His voice was taut with pain, his hands clenched the controls, his knuckles white with tension.

Compassion and a sense of shared bereavement swept over Dallas. 'I'm sorry. I . . .' If they were going to live together in peace and harmony, she'd have to be honest with him, even if doing so made her vulnerable. 'It's just that I'm so nervous.'

'Since I know how much flying you've done, I have to assume it's my being the pilot that frightens you.' His voice was cool. 'As it happens, I've had my pilot's licence since I was twenty, and the ranch bought this plane almost five years ago.' He hesitated, his face set in hard lines. 'Kyle was flying a Navy jet when he crashed. There's no comparison between that and this plane. You needn't worry—I haven't lost a passenger yet.'

'Don't be so obtuse. I'm nervous about when we get to the ranch. Our marriage. What if we fail? Living day in and day out with a stranger. Suppose I have habits you can't stand? If every time I open my mouth, you're going to be angry with me... And I've never been a mother. Maybe I won't be able to meet Nicky's needs. Is love enough? And your father... he was hardly friendly at the funeral. What if I've quit my job, married you and the judge won't let us have Nicky? This is all a horrible mistake. You should have let me take Nicky in with me. It might have been rough, but I had friends and support in Virginia. We would have managed. Here,' she waved out of the window, 'I feel as if I'm being transported to Mars.' Her voice caught. 'You can't imagine how scared I am.'

'What have you been doing? Lying awake at night thinking up problems? Quit worrying about it.'

'Easy for you to say. You probably don't have enough imagination to worry about what could go wrong.'

'Is that right? Well, if you're so much better at worrying, how come you didn't think about what we'll do if you miss the big city so much that you're miserable? Our malls and museums scarcely compare to Washington's. I've asked you to give up a lot. How do I compensate for that? What if you don't like my friends and neighbours? You've had a job that was important to you. Will you be able to find that same satisfaction out on the ranch? As for Nicky, I've never been a father. I don't know if I can even remember the prayers I said as a kid.'

Dallas stared at him in disbelief. 'You're scared, too.'

He gave her a wry smile. 'Did you think you had a monopoly on being terrified?'

She nodded. 'I'm not sure why, but somehow the idea of your being scared makes me feel better.'

'Maybe fear, like misery, likes company. At least you have the advantage over me in one area: Nicky's the spitting image of you. The same dark honey-coloured hair, the same hazel eyes with touches of golden brown and green, and the same skin that's the colour of ripening peaches. You could be her mother.'

Dallas shook her head. 'But I'm not. What if your friends and neighbours are suspicious of this marriage? Won't it hurt our chances of getting custody?'

'Why should they be suspicious? We'll tell everyone that we met at Kyle's and Alanna's wedding, met again at the funeral and discovered we had a lot in common. Nicky's a lot,' he said as she made a disparaging sound. 'I flew out to Virginia and convinced you to marry me. And every word is the truth.'

'There's truth and there's truth.'

'See that little hill over there?' Clay pointed to the east. 'It's the neck of an ancient volcano. The Spanish named it Huerfano generations ago.'

'Poor little hill. It looks so lonely and abandoned rising all alone from the plains like it does. What does Huerfano mean?'

'The orphan. Alanna used to joke that it was a fitting symbol for her and Kyle and me.' After a short pause, he added, 'Her father never tried to keep in touch with her, and when she died, we couldn't locate him. Alanna was determined that her daughter grow up knowing always how very much she is loved.'

'Just because I'm frightened of what's ahead, doesn't mean I'll back out,' Dallas said. 'You can save your pep talk.'

'Maybe it wasn't for you, but for me. Look behind us. See how Huerfano sticks out? It's visible for miles. In fact, years ago it marked the old trail from Taos to Denver. Maybe we'd do well to remember that. If we let our love for Nicky guide us, I don't see how we can go wrong.'

CHAPTER TWO

Nicky was sitting on the porch steps watching for them, her sturdy little body still encased in pyjamas although it was the middle of the afternoon. The minute Dallas and Clay stepped from the car that had come to the airfield to meet them, Nicky raced down the walk and hurtled her small body into Clay's outstretched arms. 'Where's my present?' she demanded of him.

Clay laughed and tossed her up in the air before hugging her tightly to him. 'In my suitcase. And I brought you Dallas just as I promised.' He set the child down and gave her a small shove in Dallas's direction.

Ignoring Clay's words confirming that he'd never intended to allow her to say no to his proposal, Dallas smiled down at the small girl. 'Hello, Nicky.' Even though she'd been at great pains through the years to maintain a close relationship with her cousin's daughter, and in fact had daily chatted with her on the phone since Alanna's death, Dallas wasn't surprised that Nicky was somewhat shy. Dallas gently patted the child's dirty face and held out her arms encouragingly.

Nicky accepted the embrace somewhat tentatively. 'Dallas, are you really going to live with us now?'

'Yes, I am, sweetheart. Would you like that?'

Nicky nodded. 'I think so. My mama says you're as 'pecial as I am.'

Dallas smoothed back the matted crown of dark blonde hair and hugged the warm, trembling body to her. 'Nobody is as special as you are,' she said in a teasing voice. Her nose wrinkled at the sour smell that emanated from the child's hair and body. 'Are you sick today? Is that why you're still in your pyjamas?' she asked as she followed Nicky through the door Clay was holding open.

Nicky shook her head. 'I didn't want to get dressed. Clay said I don't have to do anything I don't want to do cuz my mama and daddy died.'

Swallowing hard, Dallas said, 'And you didn't want to take a bath either.'

'I hate taking baths,' Nicky said.

'Oh, dear. That's too bad.' Dallas shrugged. 'Maybe I can find some other little girl who wants the bubble bath I bought especially for you.' From her tote bag, she pulled a large, ornate bottle mysteriously wrapped in floral paper and ribbons.

Nicky hopped up and down on her bare feet. 'No. I want it,' she cried, holding out her hands.

Dallas made a big show of doubt. 'Well, I don't know. If you don't want to take a bath . . .'

'I do. I do. Can I take one right now?'

Smiling, Dallas handed her the bottle. 'Need any help?'

'No.' The answer echoed down the staircase.

'You handled that like a pro,' Clay said in admiration.

Dallas turned to him in disbelief. 'Did you really say that Nicky doesn't have to do anything she doesn't want to do?'

'Well, sure. I mean, the poor kid just lost her parents.'

'Is that any reason to turn her into a spoiled brat?'

Clay sucked in his breath. 'She's not——'

'No. Not yet. But how long do you think it would take if everyone continued to let her have her own way? Nicky may be only six years old, but she's a bright child. She'd quickly learn how to manipulate you with only a few tears.'

He ran his fingers wildly through his hair. 'I never claimed to be an expert on children.'

'Expert! You barely qualify as a novice.' She paced across the room. 'Nicky is a sweet, intelligent, un-spoiled child. She needs us now to be strong, not weak, not giving in to her every whim. I know her parents died. That's tragic and it's tough. But if we deny her the chance to face up to what's happened, she'll never learn how to deal with adversity. Do you want her to turn out like——?' Too late she realised where her un-ruly tongue was leading her and clamped her mouth shut.

Clay grabbed her arm. 'Like her father? Is that what you're too chicken to say?'

Dallas stared defiantly up into his angry face. 'All right. I'll say it. Her father. After his accident, Kyle totally disintegrated and you know it. You and your father babied him and made him into an emotional cripple. I'm not going to let you do the same thing to Nicky.'

Clay's fingers tightened painfully on her arm. 'It must be nice to be an expert on running everyone else's lives. What do you know about how my father and I and Kyle lived our lives? You were clear across the country. All you know is what Alanna chose to tell you.' His mouth curved into an unattractive sneer. 'I notice you never turned Alanna away when she ran to you for pity.' He flung her arm from his grasp. 'What do you know about real pain and suffering?'

Dallas collapsed into a nearby chair. 'I dealt with it every day at school,' she said, her voice barely shaking. 'I know children suffer and hurt. I also know that no matter how much you love a child, no matter how much you want to protect a child, it isn't humanly possible to isolate the child from all suffering. While I can sympathise with Nicky's pain and her fears, we have to acknowledge them, not bandage over them with gifts and favours. Even a child has to be allowed to grieve. Children bounce back quicker than adults think if we simply allow them to get on with it.'

'You make it sound as if Nicky's some bug under a microscope,' he said slowly. 'How long does it take a person to grow a hard shell so that other people's suffering doesn't touch you?' He waved away the angry retort her mouth opened to give. 'You come in here and condemn me now, but where were you when Nicky got out of bed that first morning and wanted her mother and I had to tell her Alanna wasn't coming back? Where were you the evening Nicky was so upset that she threw up her dinner? Where were you when we couldn't find where Alanna had put Nicky's favourite doll? Where were you when Nicky cried all night?' Clay leaned down, his hands gripping the arms of her chair, his angry face towering over her. 'Maybe I'm not the Know-it-all Child Expert that you are, but I love Nicky, and I did the best I could. And don't you ever again accuse me otherwise.'

'I didn't mean——' Dallas began, but Clay had stomped from the room. She clutched her hands tightly in her lap, glad that Clay wasn't there to see how they trembled. She made a sound, half sob, half laugh. 'Our first day of marital bliss.'

The long days that followed were hardly any improvement. After undergoing countless interviews and hours of imagining the worst, the actual hearing giving custody of Nicky to her and Clay was relatively short and prosaic. The judge absolutely beamed at them when he discovered they were married, proving that Clay's belief that the judge was opposed to single parents had been well-founded.

So here she was. A new home. A new husband. A ready-made family. And she'd never been lonelier in her life. Nicky was the only bright spot in her days. Fortunately Clay's spoiling had been so short-term that, except for the occasional tantrum, Nicky was reverting to her normal, sweet-tempered self. But Dallas couldn't tie the child to her side. The future stretched bleakly ahead of her. Hours, days, weeks, months of time to fill and no one to share her thoughts, her dreams. If only she had one friend. If only Clay... no, Clay had no interest in being her friend. He'd needed a mother for Nicky and she was it. Efficiently he'd filled a slot much as she'd change a burnt-out light bulb. The chore done, he thought nothing more about her.

She looked up at the mangy cow head that sneered at her from over the living-room mantel. 'Don't give me that cocky smirk, you moth-eaten behemoth. If it were up to me, you'd be reigning over the county dump, not the living-room.' Striding to the window, she swept aside heavy velvet curtains. Outside the window the relentless wind whipped up the dirt and thrust tumbleweeds against the fence. Further south the tops of the Spanish Peaks were obscured by dark, fast-moving clouds. A cold and barren land. The heavy curtain dropped back into place. 'I hate Colorado,' Dallas said, speaking loudly to dispel the lonely gloom. 'I hate cows, I hate this ranch, I hate this house, I hate this room, I hate the cold, I hate the wind, and most of all,' she glared up at the head, 'I hate you.'

'Is there anything you don't hate? Once you thought that living on a ranch might be fun.'

Dallas whirled. Clay was slouched against the frame of the door, raising small clouds of dust as he slapped his hat against long, jean-clad legs. 'I was still a child. Not everybody's cut out to be Annie Oakley.' Crossing her arms protectively in front of her, she hid her fears and loneliness behind a wall of complaints. 'A lot of people like to have neighbours, shops and restaurants within walking distance, and big city amenities only a short ride away.'

'You should have thought of that earlier. I told you before. Our marriage is not a temporary situation.' Clay's voice was cold.

'That's right. You'll need a baby-sitter as long as Nicky is around, won't you?'

'You're more than a baby-sitter. You're my wife.'

'I always thought wife was synonymous with partner. None of my married friends was shunted off to a tiny bedroom on the north side of the house where it's impossible to stay warm.'

There was a derisive lift to Clay's brow. 'You're the one who insisted you needed time to adjust to marriage and motherhood before we consummated the marriage. Change your mind?'

'No.' She walked over to the mantel and traced an invisible line with her finger. An admission of her loneliness burst from her lips in spite of her intentions. 'I merely meant that most wives know where their husbands are and occasionally have a civilised conversation with their husbands.'

'Most wives also sleep with their husbands.' His bland tone of voice failed to blunt the unexpected attack.

'I see.' Dallas felt cold all over. 'I'm being punished.'

'Not at all. I've merely been keeping out of your way so that you can settle in.'

She straightened a candle on the mantel. 'It might have occurred to you that I could use a little help adjusting.'

'It might have occurred to you to ask if you needed help. Or is the ultimate expert on child care too proud to admit that she needs help?'

'You're still angry because of what I said about Nicky and Kyle,' Dallas said. 'Your pride was hurt, and you're getting back at me. Dumping me here in the middle of nowhere. Showing up only at dinner and barely speaking to me then.'

'What do we have to talk about? Nicky is our only common bond, and you've made it quite clear I have nothing to say that you want to hear on that subject. Where is Nicky anyway?'

'At school.'

'School?' A deep frown wrinkled his brow. 'Don't you think you're rushing things a little? Did she want to go?'

Dallas thought of the frenzied sobbing, the clinging to her legs, the screaming tantrum. 'No.' Nicky's tear-drenched face wouldn't leave her mind. Dallas had spent the morning fighting the temptation to drive back into town and bring Nicky home.

'Maybe you should have waited a few days.'

'It would only get worse.' She stared sightlessly into the cold fireplace. Clay's silence accused her and pushed her to explain. 'I've dealt with such situations

as a counsellor many times. I know that hanging
around or giving in to Nicky would only prolong the
agony. I drew hands on my watch and gave it to her
so she'd know she wasn't being abandoned. When the
watch matches up with my drawing, she knows I'll be
there.'

'You know all the answers, don't you?'

Dallas hunched her shoulders defensively against
his sneering assault. 'I thought I did. I never fully
appreciated how difficult it was for the parents.' She
cleared her throat of the tears that clogged it. 'I felt
like such a monster leaving her there. She begged me
not to.'

Clay walked across the room and dropped his hands
heavily on her shoulders. 'Could it be that you're not
nearly as tough as you'd like to think you are?'

Dallas shrugged from his grasp. 'I never said I was
tough. You did, just because——'

'No.' Clay's hand snaked around and covered her
mouth. 'Let's not start that argument again.' He
chuckled softly as he drew her back against his body.
'You don't feel so tough.' The whispered words were
puffs of air against her cheek, and then the curled tip
of a moist tongue bathed the curves of her ear, sending
heat pulsating through her body. She knew she should
push him away, but Nicky's tantrum had emotionally
drained her, leaving her vulnerable. She needed
someone to hold her and comfort her. Clay turned
her stiff body in his arms and pressed warm, soft kisses
on her brow, her closed eyelids, her nose, and her
cheeks. His body heat softened her token resistance,
and her mouth trembled as his lips settled on hers.
Clay worked his magic, his kisses dissolving her bones,
until Dallas was clinging to him for support.

He lifted his head. 'Perhaps it's time to move you out of that chilly northern bedroom.'

The thinly veiled amusement in Clay's voice acted as a dash of cold water on her heated emotions, and she pulled free of his arms. A small tremor shook her spine. It frightened her that she was tempted to yield. She couldn't—not yet. How could they become lovers when they weren't even friends? Putting distance between them, she fought desperately for self-control. 'Don't go reading something into a little kiss. I've had a bad morning. Is it so surprising that I responded to the first show of friendliness I've encountered since I've been here? I would have thrown myself at anyone who acted halfway civil.'

Clay frowned. 'What does that mean? If you're not receiving the respect due my wife——'

'Respect! I've had respect up to here.' She whipped her hand past her nose. 'Mrs Dalton this and Mrs Dalton that. I'm like an honoured guest with no status. As a wife, I don't exist. My menu suggestions are ignored because the boss won't eat them. The pictures have to stay where they are because the boss likes them there. Heaven forbid I should even consider rearranging the furniture. The boss wants it this way. I had to ask Jim to drive Nicky and me to school this morning because I didn't know where you were, and only the boss has the keys to all his cars. Do you have any idea how humiliating that is?'

'OK. So I haven't been much of a success with this marriage business.' He picked up his hat. 'Extra keys for all the vehicles are in my desk. Top drawer, right. Take whichever car you want,' Clay said.

'You're sure the boss won't want any of them?'

'You might cut me a little slack, Dallas. I was a bachelor for thirty-one years. Give me some time to remember that there are other people in my life to consider these days. As for Sara and the others,' he shrugged, 'most have worked for my family a long time. Alanna didn't exactly endear herself to them, and they didn't hesitate to make it clear where their loyalties lay.' He started from the room, then hesitated in the doorway. Turning around, he surveyed the room. 'What's wrong with this room? It's always looked like this. My mother moved in here and she never changed a thing. My father would have a stroke if you moved so much as one stick of furniture.'

'Your father doesn't live here. I do. If he likes this stuff so much, let him take it over to his house. I'll carry that damned cow over there myself.'

'That damned steer,' he emphasised the last word, 'is a legend around here. He's part of the family.'

'And I'm not?'

Clay clapped his hat on his head. 'That's up to you.'

Dallas glared at his departing back. Clay had pushed her around long enough. It was time he discovered exactly what kind of woman he'd married. She headed directly to the master bedroom on the second floor. The bedroom that Clay occupied. Her first step in his education would be to exchange rooms with him. He could sleep in that Arctic bedroom. Standing on the threshold, she surveyed Clay's room. Mud-covered boots had been abandoned in one corner, an old stetson hung on one of the bedposts, and a pair of jeans were tossed across the back of a cracked leather chair. The scent of Clay's aftershave was so strong in the air that she couldn't prevent a glance over her shoulder to ensure that he wasn't behind her before she stepped cautiously into the room. Much of the floor was taken up with a bed that was covered with a patchwork of sheepskin. Losing her courage, Dallas bolted from the overwhelmingly masculine room. She'd never be able to erase Clay's presence from this room.

There were four bedrooms on this floor of the ranch house; Clay had one, Nicky slept in another, and Dallas had been assigned the third. Hearing the vacuum cleaner in the fourth bedroom, she headed there.

Sara turned off the machine at her approach. 'Yes, Mrs Dalton? Is there something I can do for you?'

Dallas took a deep breath. 'Yes. First you can call me Dallas.' She looked around at the odd jumble of furniture. 'And then you can tell me what this room is used for.'

'Nothing now. It was Clay's room until his dad moved over to the small house.'

'Well, it's going to be my room now. I'm freezing to death in that other room.'

Sara bent down to pick up a piece of lint from the floor. 'Is that what Clay wants?'

'I'm here to stay. That's what Clay wants. He has more on his mind than petty worries about how the house is run.' She hoped that was true.

The housekeeper didn't look too convinced. 'There's always the guest wing where she lived with Kyle.'

Dallas decided not to comment on Sara's refusal to use Alanna's name. 'I prefer to sleep closer to my husband,' she said coolly. Let Sara make of that what she would. 'But that does bring up a question. Why is Nicky's bedroom over here?'

'Kyle and his wife went out a lot, and Clay didn't like Nicky being all alone over there. He said it was too far away.'

'What about when Clay had evening plans?'

'He didn't go out much after Kyle came home,' Sara said. 'When he did, my daughter Kim or I came over. Or Clay's daddy came over and stayed with her.'

Dallas wondered where Clay had gone when he went out. And whom he'd gone with. She could hardly ask Sara. Not that she cared how Clay had spent his evenings before they were married. Much better to concentrate on the room. The juvenile furniture had been badly abused, and the brown curtains patterned with hunting dogs were threadbare. Warm sunshine poured through south-facing windows. Forgetting Sara's presence, Dallas thought out loud. 'Grandmother's desk would go beautifully under this window. My great-grandmother's rocking-chair could go in that corner, and there would still be plenty of room for my bed.' Regret laced her voice as she added, 'I wish I'd brought my furniture.'

'Why didn't you?' Sara asked.

'Clay said the house already had too much furniture, and he didn't know what we'd do with mine.'

Sara unplugged the vacuum. 'Plenty of room in the attic to store stuff. Don't know why Clay didn't think of that.'

Because Clay wanted me to sell my furniture, wanted me to burn my bridges behind me, making it difficult for me to leave here, Dallas thought. Out loud she said, 'I stored my things in case Nicky wants any of them later, but, since there's room, I'll call up the warehouse and tell them to send everything out here.'

'I suppose you'll want new curtains,' the older woman said with a sigh. 'And it needs painting. Clay will have to take someone off the outdoor chores for that.'

'I can paint it myself. I painted my town house. And I'll make the curtains.'

'You can sew?'

'On my salary, I had to know how to sew if I didn't want to run around the school stark naked,' Dallas said.

'Always wanted to learn how to sew. Never had the time.'

Dallas heard the uncertain note in Sara's voice and realised that what Clay had implied earlier was true. Everyone at the ranch was having as much trouble adjusting to her as she was to them. Hadn't all the years of travelling with her military father taught her anything? She'd been so focused on Nicky's problems and her own grand sacrifice that she'd never stopped to consider that perhaps everyone was waiting for her to make the first overtures. 'Sewing is easy. I'll be glad to help you,' she said.

'That would be real nice of you,' Sara said. 'You want I should have someone haul all this junk up to the attic this afternoon so you can get started?'

'Yes.' An image of Clay's face floated before her. 'No. Er—maybe we'd better wait a little on that.'

Sara gave her a perceptive look. 'Until you tell Clay, you mean.'

Dallas smiled weakly. 'It's just a formality. He won't care.'

'Lordy, Dallas, I know that. Clay's a peaceable man. Not much riles him, unless it's dishonesty or disloyalty.' Sara wrapped the cord around the machine's handle, giving the simple task much more attention than it required. 'I've known Clay since he was a small boy. He can be stubborn as a mule sometimes, but in the end he's always fair.' Sara pushed the vacuum down the hall.

Maybe, Dallas thought cynically. And maybe Sara was blinded by loyalty. She looked around the room and shuddered. Never mind Clay. Sara had called her Dallas, and the two of them had actually had a conversation. It was a start.

'Where's Nicky?' Clay asked, sitting down to dinner.

'It's almost seven-thirty. She's in bed looking at some books,' Dallas said. 'I told her I'd go up and tuck her in after we ate.'

Clay laid down his fork and pushed back his chair. 'Is she sick? What's the matter with her?'

'Nothing's the matter with her. She's six years old, and she has to get up to go to school tomorrow.' Dallas spooned gravy over her potatoes. 'Allowing her to stay up all hours and go to bed whenever she felt like it is no way to raise a child. I decided it was time to put her on a more suitable schedule.'

'You decided? Just like that?' Clay scowled across the table. 'Did it occur to you that I like having Nicky at the dinner table? That's about my only chance to see her. She's not up when I leave, and she's at school when I come in for lunch.'

'Then you'll have to change your dinner hour.' Dallas buttered a roll. 'Nicky's will be at five-thirty from now on.'

'Will it?' Clay asked, his low voice challenging her.

'Yes.' She dipped her fork into some peas. Clay must not think that he could intimidate her. 'I didn't change my whole way of life to come out here and be just another stick of furniture in this—this historical mausoleum. You said you wanted a mother for Nicky, and I intend to be one.'

'Whether I approve of your methods or not.'

Dallas folded her shaking hands in her lap and faced him across the table. 'Exactly.'

'And what's my role? To put food on the table, clothes on your back, a roof over your head and otherwise keep out of your way? That was Alanna's style. Do whatever you want and the hell with anyone else. Just how much like your cousin are you?'

She stiffened at his harsh words. 'Alanna may not have been raising Nicky the way I'd raise a child, but you know she loved Nicky.' Her voice trembling, she added, 'How can you sit there and criticise Alanna? It would take a saint to put up with all Kyle put her through, the way he abused her.'

'Is that what Alanna told you? He never laid a hand on her,' Clay said, his voice hoarse with emotion.

'There's more than physical abuse. After Kyle ditched his plane at sea he was afraid to fly again and he became an embittered man who hated himself because he'd failed, and he took his anger out on Alanna. Name-calling, jealous rages... it was only a matter of time until he started hitting her.'

'She drove him——'

'Don't give me that old excuse. A man, a real man doesn't take his failures out on those around him.'

'If you knew——'

'I knew all I needed to know,' Dallas said. 'Enough to try and convince Alanna to divorce him and take Nicky away from him.'

'Kyle would never have hurt Nicky. Do you think I didn't know my own brother?'

'Kyle changed. You and your father closed your eyes to that. He wasn't the same person after he got out of the Navy.'

'Was Alanna? Or had she always been a selfish bitch?'

'She worshipped Kyle,' Dallas said with growing fury.

'Sure. When he was the all-American hero. She was great with the "for better" part of marriage; it was the "for worse" she couldn't handle. Alanna was a scheming bitch who wouldn't have known a scruple if she'd tripped over it.'

'That's not true,' Dallas said. 'She was good and kind and generous.' Her hands clenched and unclenched in her lap. 'You knew nothing about her.'

'You were so busy worshipping the goddess that you never saw the selfish manipulator behind the beautiful façade,' Clay said through tight lips. 'You're the one who knew nothing about her.'

'Alanna may have been my cousin, but we were closer than sisters. When her mother died and her father remarried almost immediately and she came to live with us——'

'Spare me,' Clay said. 'I've heard this melodrama a million times. Jealous stepmother throws gorgeous stepdaughter out into the cold, cruel world.'

His sneering words dynamited her self-control. 'Alanna said that you hated her for taking your sainted brother away from you. Only Kyle was hardly a saint.' Her indictment reverberated the length of the table.

'No.' Clay stared down into his coffee-cup. 'He was just a man.' There was a long pause. 'Kyle had such a zest for living before he had to ditch that damned plane. Then, before he had a chance to get his life back in order, he died in the car wreck. And all those damned fools mouth stupid platitudes that he's better off dead, that at least he isn't suffering any more.'

A shocking image of Kyle as last she'd seen him seared across Dallas's brain. The laughing adventurer reduced to a shadow of his former self, the limp, the self-doubt, the sense of failure that had pervaded his every word. Few besides Clay would have been optimistic enough to dream of a future that held recovery for his brother. The pain in his voice cut through her anger, and, propelled by remorse, she left her chair. Standing behind Clay, she hesitantly touched his shoulder. 'When I was a skinny adolescent with braces and blemishes on my face, Alanna used to paint my toenails and make up my face, all the time telling me that I'd grow up to be beautiful. That's how I'd like to remember her.' She prayed that Clay would understand what she was trying to tell him.

Clay reached up and slowly squeezed the hand resting on his shoulder. 'Maybe it would be best if we left each other's memories intact. I'll try harder to keep my opinions to myself.'

'Thank you.' She returned to her chair. By the time they'd finished dinner, the silence between them had stretched to an unendurable length. Gathering her courage with the dirty dishes, Dallas asked, 'Shall I tell Sara that we are all going to be eating at five-thirty from now on?'

'Do I have any choice?' Without waiting for an answer, he added, 'So this is what married life is all about. A woman coming in and complaining about the food on a man's table and the house they live in, disrupting his whole routine.'

'It's about to be disrupted more. I've sent for my furniture, and I intend to make some changes.'

Clay followed her into the kitchen. 'And if I said I like my house the way it is?'

'Your house,' she exploded. 'Your cars. Your ranch. Your furniture. Your cow head. Your pictures. Am I eating your food, too? Drinking your water?' She slammed the plates on the kitchen counter. 'Would you like me to pay rent?'

'Damn it, Dallas. Don't be so quick on the trigger. Being married is as big an adjustment for me as it is for you. If you want to do something about the damned house, do it and quit whining about it. Just stay away from my bedroom.' Clay handed her a bowl. 'Which obviously is no hardship for you.'

'Who's whining now?'

'Don't push it, Dallas.' He leaned against a cabinet. 'Bedding a reluctant wife is one thing, responding to a challenge is something else.'

'I'm not challenging you to anything,' she said, loading the dishwasher.

'Why not? Afraid you'll lose?'

'Is that what marriage is all about to you? Winning and losing?'

'What's it to you?'

'I used to think it was sharing your life with someone because you couldn't bear not to. Now...' She shrugged and turned on the dishwasher.

'Did our marriage disrupt a relationship in your life?' he asked as they left the kitchen.

'A little late to ask, isn't it?'

'Better late than never. Well?' he prompted.

'No. How about you?'

'Nothing you need worry about,' Clay said.

'That's delightfully ambiguous.'

'I'll keep my marriage vows.' His eyes narrowed as he turned towards her. 'I'll expect the same of you.'

Dallas's heart was beating uncomfortably fast as she led the way into Nicky's bedroom. From anger at Clay's subtle threat, she told herself, not because for a moment his blue eyes had appeared darkly possessive.

Nicky smiled sleepily as they sat down on opposite sides of her bed. 'Dallas said tomorrow night you're gonna eat with me,' the small child said innocently.

Clay's eyes lanced Dallas across the bed. 'Then I guess I am,' he said.

'Dallas, too?'

'Of course. The three of us are a family now.'

Clay's words brought a lump to Dallas's throat. No matter his personal preferences, he would do what was best for Nicky. Clearing her throat, she asked, 'How about a story?'

'Yes,' Nicky said. She cuddled closer to Clay. 'Tell the story 'bout Snow and Walt.'

Dallas gave Clay a questioning look.

He grinned at her. 'Your favourite animal.'

'The cow in the living-room,' she guessed.

'The steer,' Clay said emphatically. 'This land was part of an old Spanish grant when my great-great-grandfather, Walt Dalton, acquired it back in the late 1860s. He decided to run cattle on it so he went down to Texas and gathered a herd of Longhorns. Family history doesn't dwell on how Walt gathered his cattle,' he added with a grin.

Nicky tugged impatiently on his arm. 'Tell it right.'

'Well, sirree, now, ol' Walt, he roped hisself a steer,' Clay said in a drawling voice. 'A mighty big steer. White, so Walt, he called him Snow. That thar steer, he allus had to be first. Yes, sirree, ol' Snow, he didn' figger on no man or beast gettin' in front of him.'

'The stampede,' Nicky prompted.

'Who's telling this story, you or me?' Clay asked indignantly. 'One night thar come this real gully washer. Lightning so bright them cowboys reckoned it were day already. Thunder so loud it was wors'un the war drums of a thousand 'Paches.'

'And the cows was scared,' Nicky said to Dallas.

'Them cows was so spooked they high-tailed it outta thar lickety split. Ol' Walt's horse unloaded him and lit out for Montana. Walt, he looked up and saw them cows coming and reckoned he was sure 'nuf done for.'

'But Snow saved him,' Nicky said with a big yawn.

'Yup. That ol' steer, he done let Walt ride him to safety. Some other cow-pokes 'lowed as how they wouldn't mind riding Snow after that, but Snow, he was doggoned if he would go along with their notion.' Clay looked down at the sleeping child before adding softly, 'Snow led the drive up the Goodnight-Loving trail a half-dozen times, and then Walt turned him out to pasture to enjoy old age.'

'All right,' Dallas said, switching off the light beside Nicky's bed. 'Since he's a family legend, I won't toss Snow out into the barn. That doesn't mean, however, that I want him in the living-room, either.' She slanted a quick glance at Clay. 'How about in your bedroom, since you're so fond of him?'

'How about in my office?' He stopped her in the hallway. 'Snow might get jealous in my bedroom.'

She could feel the blush stealing over her face, but she refused to rise to Clay's bait. 'That's fine with me. I'm never in there, anyway.' At her words, the gleam in Clay's eyes deepened. 'I mean, in your office,' she said quickly.

'Of course. What else could you mean?'

The barely suppressed grin on his face did nothing to cool her feelings. 'I'm going to my room. To read.'

Clay stopped her, his hand on her arm. 'Without saying goodnight, Mrs Dalton?'

CHAPTER THREE

TURNING around was a mistake. Clay's lips were level with Dallas's. How could she have ever thought his lips were thin and ill-tempered? They looked cool and inviting. The corners turned up. He was laughing at her. She looked up to meet Clay's gaze. Amusement faded from his eyes, leaving them a blue that darkened like a pond with mysterious depths. The only sound was their combined breathing. And the pounding of her heart.

Words caught in her throat. He was going to kiss her, and she wanted him to. His mouth settled on hers as lightly as a butterfly landing on a flower. Their lips barely touched, yet Dallas felt the sensation jolt through her entire body. She clutched Clay's shoulders for support. He seemed to sense her weakness and encircled her waist with his arms. Strength flowed from him into her body—a strength that was sapped by his next move as he deepened his kiss and drew her tighter against his body. The tips of her breasts were pressed against his chest. Was it only her imagination or could she feel the beat of his heart? One of his arms slid down from her waist to rest over the fullness of her hips. She took a deep breath, inhaling his scent.

Clay brought his hands up to cup her cheeks and pulled his lips from hers. 'Could it be that the marital bed you've made is growing a little lonely?' he asked.

With the question, her sanity returned. 'Definitely not.' She couldn't let him know how much the kiss had affected her.

'Too bad. Mine is. Sleep well, Mrs Dalton.' One last light touch on lips quivering with need and Clay was gone. His study door closed firmly behind him.

On her left the Spanish Peaks loomed over the valley, storm-clouds clustered around their peaks. Dallas turned down the dirt road leading to the ranch. A large hawk took to the air with powerful strokes of his outstretched wings. A small creature was snared in his talons. This land tolerated no weakness; only the strong survived. Such as Clay.

An image of the man she'd married immediately filled her thoughts. Clay's strength was the quiet, enduring kind. The type of man who moved mountains, built railroads, settled countries. The type of man who knew no obstacle. Who rolled over mountains as if they were pebbles. Who would roll over her if she didn't fight back.

Except that fighting took on a whole new meaning with Clay. She could hold her own in a war of words. It was when Clay touched her that her weakness was exposed. His arms made a mockery of her defences. And he knew it. The amusement in his eyes each time he kissed her told her that he was playing with her as a cat toyed with a mouse. She didn't kid herself that she was holding Clay at arm's length. He would stay away from her bedroom only as long as it suited him to do so.

Her hands gripped the wheel. She needed more than the physical attraction which vibrated between them. Falling in love was no longer an option for her, but a marriage could be built on the foundations of liking and respect. Clay was right when he said that, if their marriage was a mockery, it was worse for Nicky than if they hadn't married at all. Nicky. Even though the child was starting to smile and laugh again, Nicky still had her bad times. For Nicky's sake, Dallas would make this marriage work.

Her resolve was hardened by Nicky's behaviour when Dallas arrived home.

'I thought you were gone,' the little girl cried, trembling as she clung to Dallas's legs.

'Didn't Sara tell you I went to Walsenburg?'

Nicky hung her head. 'I didn't believe her.'

Dallas knelt down and wiped the tears from Nicky's cheeks. 'Sara wouldn't lie to you. Let's go inside so I can show you a sample of the wallpaper for your bedroom.'

Nicky smiled through her tears. 'Is it pink?'

'Didn't my lady specifically request pink?'

'What lady?'

'You, silly.' Dallas dumped her packages on the living-room sofa and pulled the child on to her lap. 'I also picked up some books at the library, and I might be persuaded to read them to any little girl who gives me a big kiss.'

Nicky complied with a giggle. 'I'm glad you're here, Dallas. I love you.'

'How about me?' The deep, teasing voice came from the doorway.

'Clay!' Nicky bounced from Dallas's arms to be swept up by Clay. 'You know I love you, too.'

'What's all this?' Clay looked at the packages toppling from the sofa.

'My room,' Nicky quickly explained. 'It's going to be pink. With lots and lots and lots of ruffles.'

Clay gave an exaggerated sigh. 'Living with females, I suppose I'll just have to get used to feminine
gewgaws.'

Nicky screwed her face up in puzzlement. 'What
are gewgaws?'

'Silly things that girls like,' Clay said, tickling her.

'Are you a gewgaw?' Nicky asked. 'Sometimes
you're silly and I like you.'

Dallas was unsuccessful in turning her laugh into
a cough.

Clay raised a questioning eyebrow at her. 'Something you wanted to say?'

'No. I think Nicky said it all.' Standing up, she
gathered her parcels. 'It would serve you right if I
stuck pearl earrings in Snow's ears and draped lace
around his neck.'

Clay chuckled. 'Well, as to that, ma'am, I don't
rightly reckon ol' Snow's the pearly type. Why, that
goldurned ol' steer'd prolly stampede right out of this
here room.'

'I should be so lucky,' Dallas said.

Clay shook his head sadly at Nicky giggling in his
arms. 'That's the trouble with eastern dudes. They
jus' caint seem to cotton to our western ways.'

Much the same sentiment was forcibly voiced by
Peter Dalton, Clay's father, a week later. 'Where the
hell's ol' Snow?' he roared as he walked into the living-
room looking for Clay.

Dallas stepped down from the stool she was
standing on to measure the window. 'Clay's office.
I'll get Clay.'

Clay's father was not to be side-tracked. 'I heard
you were turning everything upside-down over here,
but—but dad blast it, even Alanna never had the nerve
to move ol' Snow,' Peter said.

'Perhaps you'd like to move Snow over to your house,' Dallas said, keeping a tight curb on her temper.

'Hell, no!' Peter bellowed. 'Ol' Snow belongs here. Why, he's been hanging here since my great-grandfather's time. You're messing with an institution when you move Snow.'

'I'll get Clay,' Dallas said, tight-lipped.

'I'm here,' Clay said from the doorway. His glance clearly told Dallas that he'd warned her.

'As soon as our business is taken care of, Clay, we'll haul Snow back where he belongs. She move him when you were away or something?' Peter asked.

'My name is Dallas,' she said, irritated by Peter's refusal to use her name.

'I was here,' Clay told his father. The expression on his face told Dallas nothing.

Peter snorted. 'I know what your name is, missy,' he said dismissively before turning to Clay. 'You're not going to tell me that you like this—this . . .' Clay's father waved his arms around the room.

'It's not finished yet,' Dallas said hastily. The curtains and decades of clutter were gone, and she'd painted the walls a soft blush, but the original furniture still remained, as hers had not yet arrived from Virginia.

'Listen, missy,' Peter pointed his hat at her, 'this house was good enough for my great-grandmother, it was good enough for my grandmother, it was good enough for my mother and it was good enough for Harriet. Well?' he demanded of his son.

Dallas snapped the tape-measure between her hands. She knew all too well how Clay would answer his father.

'As Dallas said, she's not finished, so it's a little premature to say whether I'll like it.'

'Hummpf. That's what I thought. We'll move ol' Snow back right now,' Peter said, 'no matter what missy here says. She has no right to come in and start changing things.'

Dallas refused to look at Clay.

'Aren't you forgetting something, Dad?' Clay's tone was mild. 'You sold this house to me. Whether my wife changes things around or not in our house is our business.' His voice hardened. 'And her name is Dallas, not missy.'

The silence that greeted Clay's words was absolute. Dallas might have giggled at the shocked look on Peter's face if she weren't so shocked herself.

After a few minutes, Clay added, 'I rather like having Snow in my office, but if he means so much to you, you can take him back to your place.'

Peter shook his head slowly. 'No.' He turned to Dallas. 'I guess I been a widower for so long I've sort of forgotten how womenfolk feel about their homes. There used to be an old bear rug lying in front of the fireplace. My grandfather shot that bear when it came around killing calves.' He smiled reminiscently. 'It may have been family history, but that moth-eaten old rug didn't last two weeks after Harriet moved in here. Funny how I'd forgotten about that. Guess a man has to give in to the womenfolk once in a while just to keep the peace.'

Dallas bit back a sarcastic rejoinder and murmured something she hoped was appropriate.

Clay stepped back to let his father lead the way from the room. Grinning wickedly at Dallas, he said, 'He meant that as an apology, you know.'

'It sounded as if he were throwing a bone to his dog,' she said. But she was talking to Clay's back as he followed his father. None the less, there was a warm glow in her stomach—along with a nagging sense of guilt. Clay had taken her side against his father. Not because he agreed with her. No, Clay had sided with her because he felt obligated to do so as her husband. And the trouble with obligations was that they were sometimes so two-sided. Clay had demonstrated his belief that a husband owed allegiance to his wife. Which raised the point—what did a wife owe her husband?

The question disturbed her throughout the day. Driving Nicky home from school, joining in the conversation at dinner, Nicky's bath and bedtime ritual— all the usual activities were only the background for a truth which pounded painfully and unceasingly at her. Being Clay's wife was more than signing her name Dallas Dalton or redecorating his house or overseeing his diet. A marriage could not sustain itself merely through conversation at the dinner table.

The problem was, once she'd shared Clay's bed, her life would no longer be the same. The act of love would be the same as locking the door to her gaol cell. Even saying her vows in Las Vegas there'd been the sense that the marriage was somehow illusionary and temporary. Sharing Clay's bed would make their marriage an irrevocable reality, but she could no longer evade making that final commitment.

Dallas gloomily looked around her new bedroom. The half-finished aspect of the room with its freshly painted walls and scarred juvenile furniture seemed to mirror the schizophrenic nature of her marriage. Legally joined as husband and wife, but physically still strangers to each other. Clay's defence of her today had seemed earth-shaking to her, and yet he'd acted as if he'd done nothing out of the ordinary. Dallas hung up her clothes and pulled a flannel gown from under her pillow, shivering in the chill of the night. Crawling between the icy sheets, she heard Clay's footsteps ascending the staircase. He passed her door without pausing. Why wouldn't he? Hadn't she stressed again and again that she wasn't ready for theirs to become a real marriage? Having made the momentous decision to consummate their marriage, it hadn't occurred to her that she'd neglected to consider one little detail. Clay wasn't a mind-reader to know that she had changed her mind.

Dallas curled into a ball beneath the covers. There was only one way for Clay to know what she had decided. She would have to tell him. Tomorrow, perhaps . . . She closed her eyes. Almost immediately she could see her father standing before her, erect in his blue uniform, his eyes registering understanding at the same time as he recognised her shirking. 'Do you really think it will be any easier tomorrow, Dallas?'

She tossed her covers aside, grumbling inwardly. That was the trouble with being raised by parents who believed in duty and responsibility, no matter how unpleasant. Her image in the mirror scowled back at her. Clay would no doubt be thrilled to be joined in bed by a icy-footed, reluctant wife who was dressed like someone's grandmother. She started towards her bedroom door. No, darn it. If she had to face the firing squad, she'd do it with her head held high.

Hidden deep in one of the drawers was the perfect nightgown. She lifted out the filmy wisp of flame-red. Alanna had spotted the négligé in Garfinckel's on one of her visits back to Virginia to see Dallas. She'd insisted on buying it for Dallas in spite of Dallas's protests that she'd never have occasion to wear such an expensive, provocative gown.

The gown had been tucked away unworn. Until now. Dallas quickly slipped the silky fabric over her head—a perfect fit. Not that there was much fabric to fit. Brushing her hair over her shoulders, she debated about wearing her robe. Goose-bumps were hardly seductive, but then, neither was chenille. In the end she left the robe and her furry slippers behind.

Light showed from beneath Clay's door as she moved quietly across the hall. The small sounds coming from his room ceased the instant Dallas knocked. Her knuckles were still in contact with the door when Clay pulled it open. The toothbrush in his hand made her want to giggle. The sight of his chest, bared to the waist by a loose-hanging, unbuttoned shirt, drained the stiffening from her knees. She struck a sultry pose against the door-jamb, as much for support as for theatrical effect.

Clay's mouth twitched. 'Something I can do for you?'

'Yes.' Had his voice always been that deep? And that gleam in his eyes... She moved one hand from behind her and toyed nervously with the ribbon tied beneath her breasts. 'I thought maybe...that is...it seemed to me...' Her voice died away as Clay's gaze took in what she was wearing, and his face seemed to freeze before her eyes. Taking a deep breath, she tried again. 'I'm trying to tell you that I'm willing——'

'So I see. I'm not.'

His clipped rejection smacked her across the face, the blood racing to her cheeks. Confused by his words and tone, she stammered, 'But—but...you said...I-I thought you w-wanted...'

'A duty visit?' Clay sneered. 'Is that what you thought I wanted? I backed you today so you're going to repay me by sacrificing yourself on the altar of obligation. Is that it?'

Dallas shook her head under the unexpected barrage of angry words. 'N-not exactly. I-I thought, that is...'

'You thought I'd be grateful if you tarted yourself up and appeared at my door. What was I supposed to do? Fall at your feet and worship them?'

'No. Just warm them.' Her small attempt at humour fell flat as Clay's eyes narrowed.

'Try slippers.' His eyes sliced over her. 'Why are you wearing Alanna's gown? Is this some new diabolical punishment you've come up with? Or are you wearing a dead woman's clothes to shame me into increasing your allowance?'

'Allowance!' she cried, momentarily side-tracked. 'I'm not your teenage daughter, I'm your wife. Whether you want me or not.' She threw back her head, her gaze locking defiantly with his. 'And this happens to be my nightgown.'

'Don't lie to me.' Clay grabbed her arm, pulling her close to his body. 'I've seen Alanna wearing it.'

'This isn't Alanna's,' Dallas protested. Then she remembered that Alanna had purchased a twin of the négligé for herself. 'She had one like it,' she said, struggling to free herself from Clay's grasp. Suddenly his words penetrated her anger and she stared up at him suspiciously. 'How do you know that Alanna had a gown like this? When did you see it on her? It's hardly a garment she'd wear to the breakfast table.'

Clay's face went blank, his body froze. 'Leave the past alone, Dallas. It has nothing to do with you.' His

hand dropped from her arm. 'You're shivering. Go back to bed.' He pointedly held the edge of the door.

Dallas fled for the sanctuary of her room. How dared Clay treat her like that? How dared he taunt her with refusing to share his bed and then, when she consented to do so—grudgingly...? It wasn't as if she had the slightest desire to sleep with him...

Admittedly, there had been a moment when she'd forgotten that theirs was not a match kindled by desire. Maybe she had been the tiniest bit curious to see if Clay's skin felt as silky as it looked... The way he'd flaunted that mat of chest hair that thinned as it dipped towards his belly before disappearing beneath the band of his trousers...

The memory sent a heated flush over her body, and she restlessly kicked aside her covers, despising her weakness. Much better to remember the contempt in Clay's eyes as he'd dismissed her. His cruel accusations. Anger, humiliation and horror warred with each other within her breast. All overlaid with a sense of sorrow and loss. An enormous chasm opened at her feet, a chasm that separated her from her husband. Would they ever be able to bridge it? The dark blanket of night smothered her beneath its oppressive folds.

Clay came into the kitchen the next morning as Dallas was making breakfast for herself and Nicky. Normally he ate with Sara and her early-rising husband at their place. 'Want some?' Dallas asked, pinning a bright smile on her face and pointing to the porridge. She had no desire to rehash the events of the previous evening.

'I already ate. Last night——'

'Was a mistake. It won't happen again. Drink your juice, Nicky, or we won't get to the corner in time for the school bus.'

'My tummy hurts,' Nicky complained.

'Maybe she'd better stay home today,' Clay said.

'I may be stupid about some things,' Dallas said, 'but I'm right about this.' She set a bowl of warm cereal before the small girl. 'I know you're worried, but you've always liked taking the bus before. And I'll be at the corner to meet the bus when you get home.'

'I just wanted to say that——' Clay began.

'That you understand riding the school bus after all this time might be a little scary. So do I, but Nicky knows that I can't drive her all the way to town every day.' She squeezed Nicky's shoulder in passing.

'I'll take her in if you're busy,' Clay said.

'That's not the point,' she said, glaring at him. Forcing a smile to her face, she said to Nicky, 'When you come home we can talk about what kind of day you had, but now you need to eat fast. Time's a-wasting.'

'If Mama was here, she'd drive me,' Nicky said.

'Your mama would agree with me,' Dallas said.

'Dallas. Listen to me,' Clay said. 'You took me by surprise.'

'Then we were both surprised. Now run upstairs and brush your teeth, Nicky, and no dawdling.' Dallas turned on Clay the minute the child was out of hearing. 'Are you deliberately trying to sabotage my efforts to help Nicky resume a normal life?'

'I was trying to help. I can't imagine why I thought you might want my help. I guess it slipped my mind that you know all the answers.'

'That's right. And now, if you'll excuse me, I have to drive Nicky to the school bus.'

'Damn it, Dallas, I came in here to apologise for last night.'

'How foolish of me not to recognise that. I assumed you merely wanted to point out more of my shortcomings.'

Clay slapped a chair out of his way. 'The hell with it.' Standing in the doorway, his back to her, he snarled over his shoulder, 'We're invited to a party Saturday night. I thought it would be a chance for you to meet some of the neighbours.' He slammed out of the door before she could reply.

By the time the school bus roared down the highway, a reluctant Nicky on board, Dallas was exhausted. Her lack of sleep the previous night didn't help. Making a U-turn, she headed back to the ranch, a cloud of dust trailing her. Behind her, the Spanish Peaks seemed to be spitting huge, puffy clouds into the heavens. The sky ahead of her was clear and blue.

As blue as Clay's eyes. Dallas's own eyes smarted with unshed tears and a sob caught in her throat. She knew that Clay had been trying to apologise this morning for his behaviour last night, but his rejection was still too raw and painful for her to forgive him. Ahead of her, red-winged blackbirds exploded into the air as the car passed a small, willow-lined creek. The red flashing on their shoulders was a bitter reminder of the gown she'd donned to seduce her husband. Anger welled within her as she remembered how guilty she'd felt the day before over her reluctance to consummate their marriage. She'd gone to Clay for his sake, not hers. He was the one who'd insisted that Nicky needed parents that were married in every sense of the word. He'd only wanted to satisfy his own selfish desires. How ironic, then, that when Dallas had overcome her reluctance, he'd discovered that he couldn't abide the thought of her in his bed.

Her jaw clenched in firm resolve and she thrust aside the utter humiliation of Clay's rejection. Never again would she allow him to manipulate her emotions. Never again would she allow him to persuade her that Nicky's happiness was contingent on their sharing a bed. From now on her marriage was nothing more than a formality. All her energy would be directed towards being the best mother that she could be for Nicky.

The night of the party was bitterly cold, and Dallas climbed quickly into the warmed car. Only the sound of the engine disturbed the silence as they drove along. The stars were bright and the Big Dipper hung low overhead. Isolated ranch houses beamed lonely pinpricks of light against the black hills. A deer appeared from nowhere to dash recklessly in front of them, his tail flagging white as he leaped the fence beside the road. A rabbit froze in the beam of the car headlights. Dallas thought of a hundred conversational topics but all died unsaid.

'How long are you going to be mad?' Clay finally asked. 'I tried to apologise. Don't you think you've given me the silent treatment long enough?'

Dallas stirred uneasily. 'I'm not mad.' She knew the words were true as soon as she said them. Several days of rehashing events in her mind, of vowing to ignore Clay, even of knowing she was in the right had been cold comfort. Anger had faded, leaving her hurt, empty, and a little sad, but no longer mad with Clay. He was as imprisoned as she was in this loveless marriage. Taking a deep breath, she asked, 'What do you want to talk about?'

'Tell me about your job. How you solved kids' problems back in Virginia.'

'I didn't solve their problems. I tried to teach them how to solve the problems themselves. Otherwise, they'd simply keep coming back with the same problems.'

'It's kind of hard to believe elementary school kids can have problems bad enough that they'd need to go to a counsellor.'

'Tell that to the children caught in the middle of divorces or to the ones suffering from abusive situations. Or to the ones who need to learn about drugs or how to deal with peer pressure.'

'Drugs? In grade school?'

'Some kids have to grow up fast these days.'

'Maybe in the big city——'

'Everywhere. Even in Colorado. Growing up is hard work.' She stared straight ahead into the night, her thoughts turning into words. 'And when you grow up, you still don't know all the answers.' Panic suddenly rose in her throat at the thought of the problems that lay ahead of her. How many more were concealed in the fabrics of their lives, waiting to ambush her? This party, for instance. She gripped her hands tightly in her lap. How many of Clay's friends and neighbours knew or suspected that she and Clay had married solely to provide a home for Nicky? Would they understand and accept her? Kyle and Clay belonged here. She was as much an outsider as Alanna had been, and Alanna had never considered herself welcome here. Dallas knew exactly how Nicky's tummy had felt the other morning when Dallas had insisted that the child ride the bus. The difference was, once the child had faced up to her fears, they had evaporated. Dallas doubted very much if this party and Clay's friends and neighbours were going to evaporate. Neither did she think that Clay would believe a stomach-ache.

He obviously believed, however, that Dallas was quite capable of taking care of herself. After introducing her to the woman giving the party, Clay disappeared. Almost immediately more arrivals claimed their hostess's attention, and Dallas found herself standing alone. All around her was the buzz of conversation as friends greeted each other and formed into small groups. Dallas felt an alien in a strange country. At her first opportunity she slunk off to an abandoned sofa in the corner where she felt it was less obvious that she was an outsider. The evening threatened to be endless.

'So you're Alanna's cousin. That Clay, he sure manages to land on his feet.' Smiling warmly, a man sat down beside her and draped his arm on the sofa behind her.

Dallas was grateful for the show of friendliness. 'Did you know Alanna well?'

'Not as well as some, if you get my drift.' He winked at her.

'I'm afraid I don't,' Dallas said.

'C'mon, honey. Alanna's cousin from back east . . . you've been around.' His hand dropped down to brush her shoulder. 'How about you and I sneak out for a cigarette?'

Dallas edged away. 'I don't smoke.'

He chuckled. 'Who needs to know that?'

Desperately Dallas looked around for Clay. He was nowhere in sight. 'I would like a drink,' she said. 'Would you mind?'

He jumped up. 'A Martini, right? I know just how Alanna liked them.'

The second he left the room, Dallas was on her feet. What kind of friend was this man to Clay that he'd try to seduce Clay's brand-new wife? Unless he knew that Clay wouldn't care. Because he knew that Clay had only married her for Nicky's sake. Her first impulse to seek protection from Clay died away. Hesitantly she joined a group of women, hovering on their outskirts, pretending she was one of them, smiling when they smiled, ignoring the hurt that grew in her breast. When the man returned with two glasses she moved closer to the women. The man scowled at her and slammed one glass down and left the room. Dallas sighed in relief.

One of the women turned a sharp eye in her direction. 'What do you think, Mrs Dalton?'

'Please, call me Dallas. Think about what? I'm afraid I-I wasn't listening.'

The woman sniffed. 'No, I suppose not. Neither was Alanna much interested in heating up vegetables.' Her voice emphasised the last word.

Dallas smiled hesitantly. 'I'm afraid that Alanna wasn't very adept in the kitchen.'

The woman gave her a scorching look. 'It was the bedroom where your cousin excelled. As you, no doubt, are well aware.'

There was a murmur of disapproval from the other ladies, but Dallas ignored them, drawing herself erect and staring coolly at the outspoken woman. 'I respected my cousin's privacy.'

The woman snorted. 'Your cousin never gave a damn about being private, so why should we? She flaunted herself and her affair——'

'Liz,' one of the other ladies broke desperately in. 'There's no call to be rude. What will Dallas think of us?'

'The same thing her cousin did, no doubt. That we're a bunch of country bumpkins too backward to know what's going on. You know as well as I what Kyle put up with. His wife and his own flesh and blood. I'm surprised that Clay——'

The other ladies managed to stem the woman's revelations, but Dallas walked away, her heart pounding painfully in her chest. The woman had accused Alanna of having an affair. The other women had tried to hush her, but they hadn't denied the truth of her remarks. Alanna and Kyle's own flesh and blood. Who could she mean but Clay? His behaviour the other night suddenly took on new meaning. He'd recoiled from Dallas in the red nightgown. Not because of a reluctance to bed a wife he didn't love, but because the nightgown reminded him of Alanna. No wonder he'd refused to discuss the subject with Dallas.

Other conversations echoed in her mind. Sara, saying Clay hadn't gone out much since Kyle had returned. Hadn't gone out because the woman he loved lived in his home? The fact that Clay had asked her to marry him because he said there was no one else. Why not? Why wasn't there another woman? Because he'd been devoting himself to Alanna? And finally, Clay describing Alanna and her exotic appearance, her milky white skin. Hardly the words of a dispassionate observer. How could she have been so blind? Here, then, was the reason Clay's friend had felt free to make a pass at Clay's wife. Along with every other person present, he was well aware that Clay couldn't care less about Alanna's cousin. The one who looked like a farmer's daughter.

Clay and Alanna. Were they actually lovers or had they been content with looks and sighs? It was obvious that her crude informer thought the worst.

Lovers. Clay had set up the perfect smokescreen with his constant condemnation of Alanna. No wonder he could hardly bear to say Alanna's name. Did he blame her for a temptation he'd been unable to withstand? He must be suffering the torment of the damned to have betrayed his brother. And then to have lost his lover.

Clay had ordered her to leave the past alone. She wasn't sure that she had the strength to do so. She didn't love Clay, and whatever had happened had taken place before their marriage. There was no reason for her to feel personally betrayed. And yet she did.

CHAPTER FOUR

'You must be Clay's new wife. I'm Mercedes Irving.'

Dallas turned in surprise. The woman studying her was a beauty with blue-black hair that hinted at her Hispanic ancestry, as did her perfect olive complexion. The name tugged at her consciousness. Mercedes Irving. 'Oh, you're the woman...' Dallas swallowed the rest of the sentence in embarrassment.

'I suppose Alanna told you I jilted Clay.' The woman shrugged. 'It's true I broke our engagement.'

'Why did you?'

'Kyle came home.'

The simple statement spoke volumes. Mercedes Irving was a woman for whom the love of one man had been the centrepiece of her life. 'But he was married,' Dallas protested weakly.

Mercedes shrugged. 'One cannot control love. To my sorrow, I know this well.' The woman's words were all the more dramatic for having been spoken in a matter-of-fact voice. Sadness lurked deep within the dark brown eyes. 'Your marriage came as a surprise, but it is good for the little girl, I think. I thought perhaps I should marry Clay and care for Kyle's child, but this is best. I hated her mother passionately. She was not a good wife. Kyle needed a woman who believed in him, not one who attacked his masculinity. He should have married me. He would have married me had he not gone away to the Naval Academy and been bewitched by her.'

The woman's astonishing disclosures coming so close on the heels of her earlier shocking discovery left Dallas unable to speak. Deep within her, anger began to grow. Privacy, decency... were such concepts foreign to these people? How casually they spoke of infidelity.

Mercedes must have seen the gathering storm-clouds on Dallas's face. 'Why are you so angry? Alanna was not a woman to remain long without a man. Besides, it is past.' She shrugged. 'I am left with my memories. You have Clay. He is a good man. A man of the earth. Dependable.'

'If Clay is so wonderful, why did you try and take Kyle from Alanna?'

Exquisite brows rose at Dallas's question. 'I did not try. I did. Kyle was in my blood. I thought that I could substitute him with Clay, but night and day could not be more different than those brothers.'

If she shrugs once more, I'm going to slug her, Dallas thought. Luckily the other woman turned away as someone called her name.

'Hello, Alanna's little cousin. Welcome to Colorado.' Another man wrapped his arm around her waist.

Dallas said something rude and broke loose of his grasp. In the next hour it seemed to her as if almost every male at the party made a pass at her. Except Clay. He was apparently in the barn looking at a sick calf. Dallas's stomach-ache had gone from imaginary to real. If she didn't get out of here soon, she was going to further embarrass herself by throwing up.

Finally Clay returned. He smiled at the hostess in a way he'd never smiled at his wife. Dallas walked up to him and grabbed his arm, cutting off the woman's conversation in mid-stream. 'I don't feel well. I want to go home.'

'Right now?' Clay asked.

'Oh, dear, I'm so sorry.' Concern darkened the woman's eyes.

Concern? Or anticipation? They must all be waiting for her to leave so they could feast on their loathsome gossipy titbits, Dallas thought cynically. 'Now,' she said.

'If you'd like to lie down...?' the woman offered.

In your bedroom? With your husband? Dallas wanted to shout. Why? So you can find out what my cousin saw in my husband? Out loud she merely said, 'No, thank you. I think I'll be better off in my own bed.'

'That's true. When I'm sick I hate being away from home. I do hope it's nothing serious.'

The woman almost sounded as if she meant it. Dallas gave her a weak smile before following Clay, who'd gone after their coats.

'Not leaving, are you, honey?'

Dallas couldn't even remember the name of the man who put his arm around her. If she could just get out of the door without starting a scene... 'Yes. I'm not feeling well.' She tried to ease out of his embrace.

'I knew there was something the matter,' he said. 'Alanna was never snooty.' He squeezed her shoulders. 'Maybe we can get together for coffee or something when you're feeling more perky.'

Dallas closed her eyes. 'I don't think so.'

'You sure don't look much like Alanna,' the man said.

'My wife is nothing like Alanna.' Clay's voice was cool behind them.

Dallas moved automatically to put her arms into the coat Clay was holding, barely listening as he bid the man goodbye.

Clay said nothing as he escorted her to the car. The interior was freezing, and Dallas shivered, attempting vainly to find warmth as she curled up inside her heavy coat. Clay reached in the back seat for a blanket which he flung over her. He hadn't said a word to her since she'd insisted on coming home. She glanced over at him. He was fussing with the heater dials. The silence ripped at her nerves. 'Why didn't you warn me?' she asked. 'Or is a little sadism your idea of a good time?'

'I don't know what you mean,' he said. 'I hoped you'd get to know and like my neighbours.'

'Is that why you just dumped me there?'

'Buck had a calf——'

'Who was obviously much more important than a mere wife.'

'I take it you didn't have a good time,' he said in a tightly controlled voice.

'A good time!' Her voice was pitched dangerously high, and she took a deep breath. 'The women are vultures, and the men are old lechers.'

'I don't know what happened——'

'I'll tell you what happened. Your good friends are a bunch of grown men who pawed at me as if they were animals.' She shuddered. 'Does everyone here have the morals of an alley cat?'

'Aren't you exaggerating a little?'

'Exaggerating! I've never felt so unclean in my life. How Alanna put up with——'

'Alanna was adept at playing games. Flirting. A few stolen kisses here and there. She added a little spice to their lives.' He carefully negotiated a corner. 'Everyone knew it didn't mean anything.'

She looked at him in horror. Why couldn't Clay admit his love for Alanna? Dallas would try to understand and perhaps their shared loss and their love of Alanna could be a thread that bound them together. If Clay would be honest, they might bridge the gulf between them. Instead, his refusal to speak was a wall that kept them apart. 'I can't believe you're speaking that way about Alanna,' she said finally in a tight voice.

'Don't you think it's time you faced the truth about her?'

'Why don't you tell me the truth?'

Clay didn't answer for a long moment. 'I think we ought to let it be. You and Alanna are so different.' He paused. 'It never occurred to me that anyone would expect you to behave as she did.' He gave her a swift glance. 'I'm sorry about tonight. There's a lot more to this marriage stuff than I'd anticipated.'

'It's a little late for second thoughts.'

'It's never too late,' Clay said.

They were back at the ranch. Dallas bolted from the car and ran inside. Let Clay thank his father for baby-sitting. Pausing only to check on Nicky, Dallas went straight to her room. Not even bothering to wash her face, she dragged her flannel nightgown over her shaking body.

Apparently it was no secret in Clay's crowd that Clay and Alanna had been having an affair. Why hadn't Alanna told her? They'd never kept secrets from each other before. Dallas wiped an impatient hand across her damp cheeks and climbed beneath the bedcovers. And Clay...didn't she have the right to know that there had been something between him and her cousin? Maybe it had nothing to do with the fact of their marriage. Maybe it had nothing to do with the fact that Nicky needed a mother. But surely he could see that it would have been better for Dallas to have known it ahead of time.

Dallas squeezed her eyes tightly, wishing she could blot out the future as well as the past. Clay couldn't bring himself to sleep with her. He'd abandoned her at the party, and now... claiming it wasn't too late to have second thoughts about their marriage. After she'd given up her entire way of life at his bidding. She'd leave him to his memories of Alanna if that was what he wanted, but she wasn't leaving Nicky. Even if Alanna had been Clay's lover, she'd still wanted Dallas to care for Nicky.

Alanna, Dallas cried softly, how could you? The conversation with Mercedes Irving came back to her. Mercedes had made it plain that she'd broken her engagement with Clay to have an affair with Kyle. Was that why Clay and Alanna had turned to each other? Two lonely people spurned by those they'd loved? Two healthy, attractive people living in the same house, one a jilted bachelor, the other a wife who must have found life insupportable with an abusive husband. Alanna had refused to leave Kyle because of Nicky. Next to Kyle's crippled mind and body, had Clay's blatant masculinity proved too tempting for Alanna to resist so that she had sought comfort in Clay's arms? Alanna had always had such a need to be loved. Drawn by thoughts of her cousin, Dallas tossed aside her covers and reached for her bathrobe, then padded down the corridor.

The bedroom had been shared by Alanna and Kyle, but Alanna's was the personality imprinted on it. A dozen photos framed in silver and brass covered the bureau top. There was a picture of Alanna and Kyle on their wedding-day and a picture of Kyle in front of his jet. The rest were pictures of Alanna with Nicky or Dallas. Dallas picked up one such photo. Taken years earlier, it showed she and Alanna standing in front of the White House, Alanna's arm around the younger girl. Another photo showed Dallas helping Alanna get dressed for the wedding. Dallas's mother had suggested that Dallas might be too young to be maid of honour, but Alanna had insisted. A tear fell on her hand. Here they were on the beach in Florida when Kyle had been stationed there. Alanna was making faces for the camera, but nothing could detract from her beauty. Another portrayed Alanna holding Nicky, love for her baby illuminating Alanna's face.

Dallas sniffed and looked around for a tissue. Clay handed her a large handkerchief. 'Where did you come from?' she asked.

'I was looking for you.'

Dallas blew her nose. 'Why? What do you want?'

'Nothing. I was concerned about you. I know the party upset you.' He looked at the pictures. 'Alanna really loved you and Nicky.' He picked up a photo. 'Why do you punish yourself by coming in here? Wishing won't bring Alanna back.'

'I know,' Dallas said, her voice muffled by his handkerchief.

'Poor baby.' Clay's voice was unexpectedly tender. 'You did have a miserable time tonight, didn't you? If you could see yourself…puffy eyes, red nose, and,' he bent his head, 'I have this uncontrollable urge to kiss you.'

The kiss was a gentle one, the barest hint of his lips pressing against hers. Dallas swayed beneath the impact. Clay immediately slid his hands from her shoulders and linked them behind her waist. He was holding her so loosely that she could have stepped from his embrace. Her every instinct warned her to flee, but her legs seemed to have forgotten how to move. She was hurt and bewildered and in need of comfort. Suddenly the past didn't matter. What mattered was that Clay's arms offered solace. Like a child, she huddled against him.

Clay pressed a small kiss in the corner of her mouth, and then his lips were exploring her entire face. 'You have salty cheeks,' he said. His tongue rasped against the sensitive skin below her ear and traced her chinline.

Dallas turned her head, searching for his mouth, but he had found the pulse at the base of her neck and was pressing his lips against the wild beat. She felt light-headed and trembly and warm and tingling. Clay abandoned her neck and she opened her mouth to protest, only to moan with pleasure when his warm tongue slipped between her parted lips. She slid her hands downward and unbuttoned his shirt so she could explore his chest. His skin was warm and satiny, while his crinkly hairs tantalised the skin of her palms. The urge to feel those same sensations against her own chest grew within her.

Clay was a mind-reader. He began to slide the heavy robe from her shoulders. Then stopped. 'Not here,' he said in a hoarse voice, and swept her up into his arms.

The covers on her bed were still tossed back and the bed's bottom sheet was freezing when Clay laid her down. Dallas shivered from the loss of Clay's body heat. 'It's cold,' she said, bewildered by the storm of conflicting emotions that battled within her.

'I'd like to stay.' Clay's eyes were dark and enigmatic.

Dallas hesitated. Clay was perfectly capable of persuading her to do his bidding, but instead he was holding back, insisting that she make her own choice. His forbearance irritated her. She didn't want to think—she only wanted to feel.

At her lack of response, Clay straightened up and whisked the covers over her chilled legs. One hand lightly touched her shoulder. 'Goodnight.'

Suddenly Dallas couldn't bear the thought of his leaving her. Arguments against deepening their marriage were forgotten. Weren't they husband and wife? He was right. Whatever had taken place in the past had nothing to do with them. Not now. She caught at the hand that lingered on her shoulder. 'Stay.'

'Are you sure?' He leaned over the bed, one hand playing with the belt of her robe.

Dallas could scarcely breathe, much less answer. She trailed her fingers over his hand and then pressed his fingers to the belt's knot. 'I-I . . . yes.' The mattress sagged beneath his weight, and then Clay spun her into a world of pleasure and sensation.

The sound of her bedroom door closing awakened Dallas. The room was dark with no hint of morning invading her windows. Dallas squinted at the clock on her bedside table. Three a.m. She didn't have to roll over and look to know that she was alone in bed.

The room was chilly and she pulled up the blankets so that only her nose was exposed. Beneath the covers her body felt foreign to her. Last night had been one of discovery—of new sensations, desires, reactions. Clay had been a patient lover. She was the one who'd been impatient. Heat coursed through her body at the memory of Clay's hands, his mouth, his body. He'd teased her for being so eager. Had that driven him away? Apparently he couldn't leave her quickly enough.

She curled her arms around her chest in misery, self-doubt flooding over her. Had Clay slept with her because he felt obligated to perform his husbandly duties? Or as a substitute for Alanna? He'd turned out the lights before entering her bed. A despairing sob rose in her throat. In the dark had Clay pretended that Dallas was her cousin?

Let the past alone, he'd said. Naturally. That was in his best interests. Couldn't the same be said of her? Did it really matter if Clay had loved Alanna? It wasn't as if he and Dallas shared a love-match. What they shared was a love for a child and an earnest desire to give that child a happy home life.

Marriage had been the first step in providing for Nicky's future. Maybe Clay was right in stressing that Nicky needed more than two people living in the same house. Dallas moved restlessly beneath the blankets. She no longer knew who was right, what was right. Whatever Clay's motives for making love...no, she wouldn't call it that. Whatever his motives had been, she must view the night as a positive step towards building the kind of marriage that she knew was right for Nicky. No promises had been made that doing so would be easy.

Although it was Sunday, Clay was gone when Dallas finally climbed out of bed. She and Nicky were discussing Sunday school when the phone rang.

'Clay asked me to call you,' Sara said. 'There's a winter storm warning for this area, and he wants you and Nicky to stay home from church this morning.'

Dallas looked out of the window. There were only a few flakes drifting down. 'It doesn't look so bad.'

'Not now. But a blizzard can strike quickly in this part of the country. Clay left early for the Downer place. He didn't know when he'd get back.'

'Downer place?'

'Some land he leases about ten miles away. He wanted to check for any early calves and get them to the barn. If we do get a blizzard, they'd freeze.'

'You said he left early. How early?' Her heart almost stopped beating as she waited for Sara's answer.

'He was over here about six for breakfast, so I guess about six-thirty. He said he didn't want to wake you, that you'd been out late to the party. How was it? Clay didn't say much. To busy feeding his face.'

'It was nice. They have a nice house.' How long before Sara heard the truth? Dallas wondered as she hung up the phone. Clay's neighbours had probably had a field day ripping apart Dallas's morals after she'd left.

During the long day Clay's advice proved to be good. Low dark clouds rolled in from the north bringing colder temperatures and ever-increasing amounts of snow. The wind picked up, howling around the eaves of the house with lonely cries. Dallas played with Nicky and read to her, but her thoughts continually returned to the previous evening. Clay hadn't left for several hours after he'd departed her bed, proving that he'd hadn't left her bed because he was worried about the weather. What would he expect of her now that they'd slept together? No mention had been made of her moving into his bedroom or Clay moving into hers.

Nicky had long ago been put to bed by the time Clay returned. His eyes were rimmed with fatigue, his shoulders slumped in weariness, his heavy jacket coated with snow. He brought with him the cold winter air. Any idea of discussing the state of their marriage was instantly forgotten. 'Have you eaten?' Dallas asked.

Clay shrugged out of his coat. 'Took some sandwiches and coffee with me. Finished them off about three.'

'There's soup left. I can heat you up some.'

'Let me grab a quick shower first.'

Soup and a grilled cheese sandwich were on the table when Clay came down to the kitchen. 'Looks good,' he said. He sat down and concentrated on the food.

The kitchen was a warm oasis from the shrieking winds outside. Blue-checked curtains, white wood cabinets, and an old-fashioned stove should have added up to a feeling of comfortable cosiness, but they didn't. Dallas watched Clay from beneath lowered eyelids. The scent of his soap reached her across the table. His gaze was fixed on his plate as he ate—as if he didn't want to look at her. Tension twisted her insides. Why didn't he say something? Even if he didn't want to talk about last night, he could make a comment about the weather, anything. The silence seemed to build in the room. 'Everything OK?' she finally asked.

Clay gave her a quick, questioning look.

'Out there. Sara said you were looking for calves.'

'Yeah. Found a few. One cow who'd just calved was in a bad way, and we had to haul her in and sew her up. I think she'll be OK.' He shoved aside his plate. 'Thanks. That hit the spot. Now, if you'll excuse me,' he stood up, 'I think I'll hit the sack. I'm beat.'

Dallas slowly gathered up his dirty dishes. Clay's behaviour could be interpreted only one way. He was sorry that last night had ever taken place. Obviously he had no intention of discussing it. She slammed shut the dishwasher door. It would be a cold day in hell before she brought it up.

Clay was in the kitchen having coffee the next morning when she came downstairs.

'I'll drive Nicky to the bus,' he said. 'The snow has stopped, but the roads are pretty tricky.'

'But I was going to Walsenburg. My wallpaper's in.'

'Jim is going to pick up some more grain cake for the cattle. He can run your errands,' Clay said.

'All right.' Dallas hoped her disappointment didn't show on her face. The day stretched endlessly before her.

Clay was watching her over his mug. 'Big plans in town?'

'No. Just something to do.' She paused. 'It's silly to have Sara come over every day. I can do the household chores and cook dinner.'

'And where would Sara find another job? Especially one so convenient to her home.'

'I didn't think about that,' Dallas said.

'Do you have any long underwear?'

She gave him a startled look. 'No.'

'I'll get some from Sara when I take Nicky. You can help me out today.' He grinned. 'Maybe it is about time we gave you some honest work to do around here.'

Dallas couldn't prevent the answering grin that covered her face. Suddenly Clay looked younger and more carefree than she'd seen him since the funeral. She was reminded of the Clay she'd met ten years ago. Another thought struck her. 'Do I have to ride a horse?'

Clay laughed. 'Can you?'

'I rode some when I was in high school. A couple of my friends owned horses. But that was years ago.'

'I don't see any problem. You're probably a regular bronc buster. I'll saddle up Dynamite for you.'

'I hope you're joking,' Dallas said.

'If you're going to be chicken, I guess we'll have to settle for the pick-up.'

Which he'd obviously had every intention of doing all along, Dallas thought, strapped in beside Clay as they careened down the icy road, the back of the truck filled with small hay bales. 'I thought cows ate grass and stuff from pastures,' she said.

'They do when they can get to it. Horses will paw through the snow for grass, but cows use their noses, and when the snow is this deep they can't get to it.' Clay stopped the pick-up to open a gate into the pasture. 'And in the winter they need supplemental feeding for nutrients.'

Dallas looked about her in delight. The valley was a winter wonderland, snow coating the bushes and trees, the mountains that rimmed the valley stark white against blue skies. Here and there dark mounds dotted the white landscape, cows with their breath smoking in the cold morning air.

'Think you can feed while I drive the pick-up?' Clay asked. 'I'd let you drive but you're such a greenhorn, you'd probably land us in a ditch or a snowbank.'

'Such confidence. I'll feed if you'll tell me what to do.'

'I'll show you.' He stopped the truck and led Dallas around to the back and boosted her up into the bed. 'Climb up to the top of the bales and use this to cut the twine.' He tossed her a small pocket-knife. 'I'll drive slow and you throw down bunches of the hay so that we leave a trail behind us.' Jumping back in the pick-up, he sounded the horn.

'What do you want?' Dallas hollered.

Clay stuck his head out of the window. 'I'm calling the cattle. Most of them have seen us and the rest will come running when they hear the horn.'

Come running was right. Dallas could see the large beasts loping towards them from all directions. The pick-up started with a small jerk, reminding her that she was here to work, not to sightsee. She quickly sliced through the string on several bales and, pocketing Clay's knife, began tossing the loose hay behind them. As Clay manoeuvred the truck around the pasture, the trail of hay and feeding animals strung out behind them like the tail of a kite. Dallas was congratulating herself on her expertise when the pick-up hit a concealed rock and the bales of hay on which she was standing teetered unexpectedly. Losing her balance, Dallas tumbled to the ground in a flurry of hay bales.

The snow and the hay broke her fall, and as the pick-up had been travelling slowly the only damage was to her pride. Wiping the snow from her face, she looked up, expecting to see Clay jumping from the truck laughing at her, but the pick-up was continuing on its slow journey. Not nearly as slow was the bull charging towards her. Dallas had fallen away from the packed trail, and the snow where she lay was deep. She struggled to stand, but she might as well have been mired in quicksand for all the progress she made. Another quick glance showed her the bull almost upon her. The sound of the pick-up's engine drowned out her yells for Clay. There was no way she could outrun the angry beast. Dallas burrowed deep into the snow, curling up in a foetal position, her hands protectively clasped over the back of her neck. There was a snorting in her ear and then hot, pungent breath seared her face. She whimpered Clay's name.

'Are you hurt?'

Relief flooded over Dallas at the welcome sound of Clay's voice. 'I'm fine,' she said. Seeing the concern on his face, she added, 'I landed in nice, soft snow.'

Clay helped her to her feet and started brushing the snow from her. 'You're sure you're OK?'

'Yes, I——' Suddenly she remembered the bull and looked frantically over her shoulder. The bull was standing right behind her. 'Clay! The bull!' Her eyes riveted on the bull, she made a leaping plunge towards Clay. He wasn't expecting her move and they fell as one back into the snow.

'What the hell...?' Clay struggled to sit up.

Dallas grabbed him and tried to tunnel her way into his chest for protection. The bull nudged at her back. 'The bull!'

'What bull?'

Dallas squeezed her eyelids together. 'That one.' She thumbed over her shoulder. 'He charged me.'

Clay's body began shaking beneath her. 'Dallas, that's no bull. She's a cow and gentle as a baby.'

'A cow? Look at those enormous horns.'

Clay stood up. 'She's a Longhorn. Both males and females have horns.'

'If she's not a bull, why is she after me?'

'She's not after you. She's after the hay you're lying on.' There was no mistaking the laughter in Clay's voice.

Dallas leaped to her feet and stumbled away from the scattered hay. The cow lowered her head and started to munch the feed, totally ignoring Dallas. 'Well, how was I to know?'

'I always thought that the difference between males and females was rather obvious.' Clay shoved the cow out of his way and kicked the hay away from the drift back towards the trampled snow and spread it out. Several more cows trotted their way.

'If you're talking about people, sure. Males are the arrogant ones. Anyway, I was moving too fast to check for anatomical differences.'

'You call that fast? I could have outraced you on my hands and knees,' Clay said.

'I was slowed down by all these clothes you insisted I wear.' Plodding along at Clay's side, she added, 'I feel like the Michelin man.'

'You don't look like the Michelin man.' Clay swept some snow from her hat.

'More like the abominable snowman, I suppose.' They were back at the truck. Dallas turned obediently at Clay's gesture so he could remove the snow from her back before she got inside.

Clay turned her to face him as he brushed her front. 'Abominable . . . maybe.'

'Abominable, am I?' Dallas quickly leaned down and grabbed a glove full of snow. Before Clay could discern her purpose she smashed it in his face. A mistake. As Clay had claimed, she was much too slow for him. A flying tackle sent her face first into the snow. Even as she squirmed from his grasp, she was grabbing fresh ammunition and flinging it over her shoulders, but Clay was too strong for her. In seconds she was wiggling futilely beneath his hard body, her hands held outstretched in his above her head.

'Now we'll see whose face gets washed,' he said.

'I suppose it's too late to apologise.'

Clay leered down from his straddled position. 'Try me.'

'I'm sorry I washed your face with snow,' Dallas said.

'And?'

'And I'll never do it again.'

'And?'

'What do you mean, "and?"'

'And you're sorry you called me arrogant,' Clay said.

'If the shoe fits...' At his threatening move, she hastily shouted, 'OK, OK!' adding in a prim tone of voice, 'I'm sorry I called you arrogant.'

Clay released her hands and rolled to one side. 'Why don't I think you're sincere?'

Dallas rose to her feet and looked down at him supine on the snow. The truck was only two steps away from her. 'Possibly because I had my fingers crossed.' She scooped up some snow and flung it at Clay and then ran for the truck. Jumping inside, she locked the doors and grinned triumphantly at him.

Clay grinned back. Reaching in his pocket, he pulled out his keys and swung them in a wide arc outside her window. Dallas resigned herself to the inevitable.

'Mess with the bull, you get the horns,' Clay said in a dulcet tone as he lifted her from the truck.

'What are you going to do?'

'Revenge is sweet.' He dropped her in a deep drift of snow. Before she could scramble away, he fell on top of her, his body pressing her down into the snow.

Dallas shrieked and threw her arms around his neck, burying her face in his chest. She could feel his laughter as he tried to pull her away so he could wash her face. Knowing what was in store for her if he won strengthened her resistance. For all his success, she might have been glued to him.

Finally Clay stopped struggling with her. 'All right. You win. I won't wash your face.'

Cautiously Dallas loosened her death-grip of his neck. 'Really?' Her answer was a face full of snow. 'Cheater!' she sputtered, blinking the snow from her eyes.

Clay brushed the snow from her face. 'I had my fingers crossed, too.'

'That's not fair.' She blew away a tendril of hair that was stuck to the side of her mouth. 'You're bigger.'

'Don't you know? All's fair in love and war,' Clay said.

'But this isn't . . .'

'Isn't what? Love? Or war?'

CHAPTER FIVE

'IT'S neither,' Dallas said. Despite the cold day and the snowpack beneath her, she was warm. 'Let me up.'

'I'm much too comfortable to move. You make such a nice, soft mattress.' Clay took off his glove and trailed a finger across her cheekbone. 'You have snow on your eyelashes.' His breath smoked in the cold air, warming her face.

'I have snow everywhere.'

The remark was meant to be tart, but Clay spoiled the effect as he swallowed her words, his mouth covering hers in a deep kiss. He must have been supporting himself on his elbows because his body barely pressed against hers. Layers of clothing separated them, but instead of insulating her from him the clothing seemed to heighten her awareness of him. His fingers were warm against her face, while his tongue explored her willing mouth. Her body trembled in response.

Clay shifted his weight, rubbing slightly against her body. The mere touch was enough to swell her breasts, and Dallas could feel her nipples contract to hard buttons that strained to be free. The rough texture of lace rubbed against the sensitive tips in exquisite torture. Deep within her, another, stronger need unfurled its hot demands, and Dallas welcomed the weight of Clay's hips against hers. Need and curiosity impelled her to explore the moist recesses of his mouth with her tongue. Jolts of desire shot through her veins.

'It's snowing.'

Dallas blinked, aware of little beyond the loss of Clay's lips. 'What?'

'It's starting to snow.' Studying her face, he rubbed her lower lip with his thumb. 'You're too damned distracting,' he finally said. Springing to his feet, he reached down with one hand and pulled Dallas to her feet. 'We'd better finish up the feeding.'

She concentrated on the sky. 'Yes.' She'd never even noticed that the sun had disappeared behind ominous clouds and that a few errant snowflakes had begun to fall. Embarrassment and disappointment warred within her. She'd wanted Clay to make love to her. Even worse, as unsuitable as the time and place were, she still wanted that. At least, her body did.

Clay help her brush the snow from her clothing before she climbed into the truck. When she reached over to close the door, he held it open and gave her a wry look. 'You are abominable. And without shame.'

Dallas felt the heat rush to her cheeks. 'You started it.'

'You weren't exactly fighting me off. In another minute I'd have ripped off our clothes and we'd have got frost-bite in places we could never explain.' Back in the driver's seat, he added, 'On the other hand, we might have melted the snow.'

There was no safe answer, but Clay didn't seem to expect one. Leaving that pasture and heading to the next, he seemed content having had the last word. The inside of the truck was too warm after their exertions out in the weather. Dallas pulled the heavy knit cap from her head and shook loose her hair as Clay came to a stop in the middle of a field.

Resting his arm on the steering-wheel, he turned to her. 'Game to try again?'

'Try what?' she asked warily.

'Feeding the cows. I'll make a cowhand out of you yet.'

'Don't count on it.' Dallas was tired of feeling that she came up short out here in the west. 'Everything I do here is wrong. You should have married Mercedes. She could probably feed cows with one hand tied behind her back.'

'She probably could, but Mercedes can't stand cows.' His voice was amused. 'Her dad ranches near by and, like Kyle, she couldn't get away from the ranch quickly enough. I suppose Alanna told you. Not that it's any secret. Mercedes dumped me when Kyle returned home. She was wild for him from the time she entered high school.' Reaching across her, he opened her door. 'Hop out before we're overrun by hungry cattle.'

Dallas paused with her hand on the door. 'And so when Kyle died, you asked me to marry you instead of asking Mercedes.'

Clay gave her a mocking look. 'Spurning the woman who spurned me for the sake of revenge? What I needed was a mother for Nicky, and Mercedes never struck me as the maternal type.'

'But you were once engaged to marry her.'

Clay unleashed a slow grin that scorched Dallas clear across the seat. 'I wasn't thinking of her maternal assets when we discussed marriage.' His next question made clear the subject was closed. 'Still have the knife for cutting the twine?'

Dallas fumbled around in her pockets before successfully locating the small knife. 'Give me a minute before you honk so I'm not attacked by hungry cows.'

Clay laughed. 'Take a look. Most came running the minute they heard the truck.'

Dallas mentally groaned at the sight of the cows milling about before she scrambled from the truck. She absolutely would not let Clay know how nervous the huge beasts made her. At least this group didn't have horns. Safe in the bed of the truck, she breathed a sigh of relief.

'Try and stay closer to the centre of the stack this time,' Clay yelled out of the window. 'You keep falling out and enticing me into the snow, I'll never get my work done.' Before Dallas could reply, he whipped his head back in the window and drove slowly in a large circle around the pasture, honking the horn a couple of times.

Dallas dutifully tossed the hay to the cows following them. She was winded and ready to stop when he finally brought the pick-up to a halt. Clay jumped from the cab of the pick-up, a frown on his face. 'What's the matter?' she asked.

'That cow up there. Must be some reason why she didn't come down to feed.' Clay started up the incline, his long stride eating up the distance. Dallas struggled to keep up with him, taking two running steps to each one of his, but he quickly outdistanced her.

When Dallas, breathing painfully in the thin, icy air, reached him, he was on his knees beside the cow. She looked down. 'A baby. Is he dead?'

'Close. He was born too early. It was cold last night and this little fellow is soaked. Doesn't look like his mama was able to get him up to lick him dry.' Clay stood up, hefting the calf in his arms. 'Let's get him back to the barn.'

The cow and Dallas both followed Clay anxiously as he strode back to the truck. 'Can I help?' Dallas asked.

'If you could run on ahead to the truck and spread a little hay in the back, I'll put him on that.'

Dallas quickly did as Clay asked. 'Poor fellow,' she crooned, as Clay grabbed a blanket from the front and tossed it over the calf. The mother mooed in distress.

Clay patted the cow absently. 'Would you mind riding back here?' he asked Dallas. 'I don't think he has enough life left in him to try and jump out, but no sense taking any chances.'

The trip back to the barn seemed to take forever. Dallas petted the calf and reassured him over and over again that Clay would take care of him.

Clay drove the pick-up right up to the barn doors. 'Run up to the house and tell Sara we need some warm milk.'

Dallas rushed to do his bidding. Back at the barn with a bottle of milk, she found Clay had wiped down the calf and laid him on some straw. He was fixing a heat lamp over the shivering animal. 'Let's see if we can get him to drink,' he said.

Dallas held the bottle to the calf's mouth, but the animal was too weak to suck. Clay dropped to his knees and poured milk on his fingers. He thrust them in the animal's mouth. There was no response. He tried again.

'It looked like he swallowed,' Dallas said.

'I think you're right. Here.' He handed her the bottle. 'You keep trying for a little longer. Then let him sleep while you go in and clean up. I'll keep an eye on him. And, Dallas,' his hand rested on her shoulder, 'don't count too much on this little fellow making it. He's pretty far gone.'

'He'll make it. I know he will. Look, he swallowed again.'

Clay gave her shoulder a squeeze and left her alone with the calf. Determined to save the animal, Dallas wet her fingers again and again with the milk and forced them into the calf's mouth. Finally his eyes closed and he refused to swallow any more. Dallas caught her breath. Then she saw the sides of the small animal move rhythmically in and out. He was sleeping.

Her legs ached from kneeling on the hard floor, and she leaned back against the wooden stall and stretched her legs out in front of her. The barn seemed huge and empty around her, but then she heard a rustling sound. Mice. Giving credence to her supposition, a large tabby cat crept past the opening to the stall, ignoring her as he went about his deadly business. Male voices came from outside, too far away for the words to be distinguished. From further down the row came a stamping of feet. Another cow or a horse. Dallas was too tired to look.

She took a deep breath—a mistake. The barn's odour was all too intense for a city girl. She ought to go and bathe. Her hands were sticky with milk and her hair...between the snug-fitting knit cap and lying in the snow...and other things...it was probably a tangled mess.

She looked down at the calf lying at her side. Dealing with the animal, Clay's hands had been deft, yet gentle. It had come so natural to him to attempt to soothe the distressed mother that he hadn't even been aware of petting her. Dallas recalled the little smile on Clay's face when the calf had first swallowed.

There was a kindness, a gentleness in Clay. She'd seen the same qualities in him when he was with Nicky.

Only with his wife was such behaviour non-existent. Dallas drew up her legs and rested her chin on her knees. In normal marriages a man and wife shared the same bed. Even if all they did was sleep side by side. She understood that Clay had been tired last night. But couldn't he have said something? Anything that would have reassured her about the previous evening.

Why did she fight the obvious? There had been no promises that one night with her would magically change their marriage into something that it was not. Clay had told her that he would not satisfy himself outside their marriage. Only severe need could have driven him to her bed. She was nothing more than a way for him to keep Nicky and to meet his needs. This afternoon proved that. He'd been teasing her. The kiss meant nothing to him, merely his retribution for her washing his face with snow. He'd erased all thoughts of the snow, the cold, the discomfort, even the cows from her mind. She'd erased nothing from his. Wearily Dallas arose. A bath and lunch was what she needed. This appalling urge to bawl her eyes out was simply tiredness and hunger.

Several hours later Dallas tiptoed back into the barn with Nicky. 'Wait until you see him,' she whispered to the small girl. 'He is so tiny and cute.'

The calf was gone. Dallas could have kicked herself. How could she have been so stupid as to tell Nicky about the animal without first checking with Clay to see if the calf had survived? Hadn't Clay warned her that the animal's chances were slim?

'I'm sorry, Nicky. Clay told me that the calf was very sick. He must have died.'

Nicky kicked at the stall with her boot. 'Who wanted to see a stupid ol' cow anyway? I hate cows. If the mama loved him she would have taken care of him. She wouldn't have left him.'

'She didn't leave him, honey. It was too cold last night,' Dallas said.

'I'll bet she left him. Went to a cow party or something and didn't come home. I hate mother cows who do that. Go off and leave their babies.'

Dallas dropped to her knees and encircled the small shoulders with her arms. 'Like your mother left you.'

Nicky scuffed her boot in the straw. 'I hate my mother.'

'You're angry she left you.'

Nicky nodded.

'Sometimes I get mad, too,' Dallas said. 'I loved your mother and I didn't want her to die.'

Nicky stared at her. 'Why did she?'

The back of Dallas's throat ached as she fought tears. 'Your mama loved you so much. She didn't want to die in a car crash. Things like that just happen.'

'You're crying.' Nicky reached up and wiped away a tear on Dallas's face. 'Clay said big girls don't cry.'

'Clay is mistaken.' Dallas grabbed the small hand and pressed it to her cheek. 'It hurts very badly when people die, and lots of big girls and big boys cry.'

'Grandpa and Clay didn't cry.'

Dallas took a deep breath. 'Just because you didn't see them, doesn't mean they didn't cry. They loved your mother and father, and they miss them, too.'

Nicky threw herself into Dallas's arms. 'I don't really hate Mama. And I'm sorry the little calf died.'

'Who said he died?'

Dallas hadn't heard Clay come in. She sniffed and wiped her cheeks. 'He's not here.'

Clay glared down at her. 'Come on.'

Dallas and Nicky followed Clay to the other end of the barn where Clay lifted Nicky up to stand on the top railing of the last stall. Inside the mother cow stood placidly munching some hay. At her side, his skinny legs still wobbling, the calf was nursing noisily. 'We brought Mom in this afternoon. He'll do better out of the cold,' Clay said. His face softened. 'Hungry little cuss, isn't he?'

'What's his name?' Nicky asked.

'He doesn't have one. You can name him,' Clay said.

Once the suggestion was made, it was clear to Dallas that Nicky was going to be glued to the calf's side until she came up with the appropriate name. Knowing that Nicky would be OK with Clay in the vicinity, Dallas turned to leave.

Clay walked with her to the barn door. 'I heard your conversation with Nicky,' he said abruptly. 'Do you have to rub her nose in the fact that her parents died?'

Dallas stared at him in astonishment. 'We can't just ignore that it happened. Are you aware that Nicky believed her parents left her because they were angry that she didn't make her bed?'

'That's absurd.'

'You and I know that, but how could Nicky when no one would let her talk about what happened? Every time she tried, everyone hushed her up. She was sure what happened was her fault.'

'Is that any reason to tell her you're mad at Alanna?'

'It's the truth. I am angry with her for dying and leaving me,' Dallas said.

'It's not as if she had a choice.'

'I didn't say it was rational. I said it was how I feel. Letting Nicky think her anger was wrong would only make things worse. A child goes through stages in dealing with grief. If it's so hard for us, why wouldn't it be difficult for her? Don't you ever have moments when you are furious with Kyle for dying?'

Clay's eyes turned cold and empty. 'I'll send Nicky up to the house in plenty of time for her to wash for supper.' He turned away.

'Clay.' Dallas grabbed his arm. 'I didn't mean to...it's natural to be angry with the person who dies. It's nothing to feel guilty about.'

He shrugged off her hand. 'Who the hell said anything about my feeling guilty because my brother died?'

'I simply meant——'

'Just because you're some fancy school counsellor you think you can come out here and analyse us all and tell us how to run our lives. It may surprise you to know, Miss Know it all, that we did just fine before you ever came along so you can just keep your Freudian mumbo-jumbo to yourself.' He stomped off and was quickly swallowed up by the dark interior of the barn.

Dallas stared after him in chagrin. When would she learn to keep her mouth shut? Clay's relationships with his brother and his brother's wife were so complex, it wasn't possible to discuss either one of them without angering him. She turned towards the house with a sigh. This morning, out feeding the cows, she'd felt their marriage might have a chance. This afternoon she knew the truth—no one could compete with a memory.

Hours later Dallas tossed restlessly in her bed. If she were a witch she'd call down every evil curse she knew upon Clay's head. He was inhuman. A beast. Teasing her with kisses. Arousing needs he had no intention of meeting. If only he hadn't slept with her the other night. A person didn't yearn for what she didn't know. She wiggled her hips, seeking a comfortable position. The blankets weighed heavily on her aching breasts, and she could scarcely bear the feel of her flannel gown against skin sensitised by the memory of Clay's lips.

A shaft of light from the hall fell across her bed. Clay stood in the doorway. 'Still awake?' he asked.

'Yes.'

He shut the door. His voice came from the darkness. 'I forgot to ask if you want to help me again tomorrow.'

Before she could answer she felt the bed dip. 'I-I can't.'

'Can't? Or won't?' Clay cushioned Dallas's head on his arm. 'What happened today shouldn't happen again.'

'It's not because of some insignificant kiss. I have——'

'Who said anything about a kiss?' His mouth swooped down and captured hers, and then his tongue was persuading her lips to part. 'I was quite sure that would happen again,' he murmured after a few minutes. His fingers traced patterns on her cheeks before threading through her hair. 'I was referring to your fall.'

His head was only a shadow in the darkened room, but the amusement in his voice reached her clearly.

How unfair of Clay to tease her, knowing he could do so with perfect impunity. She'd agreed that theirs would be a real marriage, so she could hardly refuse his kisses. Not that Clay was teasing her about meeting her obligations. What amused him was the fact that she was meeting those obligations with somewhat more than stoic acceptance—a fact her husband was obviously well aware of.

The skin of his chest was warm against her palms as he leaned over her. 'Well?' he asked. 'Have you managed to come up with an adequate excuse not to come out with me tomorrow?' He outlined the neckline of her gown, flipping open the top buttons with a flick of his fingers.

She could scarcely breathe. Her pulse pounded at her throat. 'I-I wasn't aware that I needed an excuse. Maybe I just don't want to go with you.'

'Don't you?' Clay slid a hand inside her nightgown, his knuckles brushing against the swelling curve of one breast. 'Perhaps I can persuade you.' He leaned down and nuzzled the sensitive skin beneath her ear, his fingers kneading the tip of her breast.

'I have to help in Nicky's classroom tomorrow.' As Clay's lips slid downward, she quickly added, 'I promised.'

Clay chuckled softly. 'In that case...' His tongue bathed her taut nipple. 'You wouldn't want to face a room full of first-graders without a good night's sleep.' She almost cried out, thinking he meant to leave her, but then she realised his hands were busy with the rest of the buttons. 'Think of me as your sleeping-pill,' he said.

Dallas couldn't have replied if she'd wanted to. Not that she did. Not when this was what she'd been aching for all day. Clay might be an arrogant beast and self-centred husband, but there was no denying he was teaching her body to crave his. He was warm and hard and silken, his muscles flowing smoothly beneath her palms. And he was hers. The triumphant thought was fleeting as Clay's hands and mouth pulled her into the sensuous pleasures of her marriage bed.

When she awakened, the other half of her bed was empty and cold. Clay must have abandoned her hours ago.

Nicky bounded into the bedroom and jumped on the bed. 'Hurry up. You're going to school with me today, remember?'

A reluctant smile tugged at Dallas's mouth. Clay had been right about one thing last night: she'd slept like a log. Eventually. But now was not the time to dwell on that. Or on the fact that once again Clay had not stayed the night with her. 'Don't tell me to hurry when you're still standing around in your PJs,' she said to Nicky. 'Get the lead out, kiddo.'

Nicky ran giggling from the room, and Dallas loosened her death-grip on the covers she'd been holding up to her neck. Explaining her nakedness to the child was more than she could handle at the moment.

Nicky precipitated the crisis at the dinner table that evening. 'Dallas is gonna be a teacher,' she announced to Clay.

'You mean she helped your teacher today,' he corrected her.

'Gonna be a teacher. Mrs Gomez said so.'

Clay turned to Dallas, a frown on his face. 'I'm sure there is a reasonable explanation for Nicky's misunderstanding.'

'There's no misunderstanding.' Dallas concentrated on pouring Nicky a glass of milk. 'I intended to tell you later this evening. Today brought home to me how much I miss my job.'

'You knew the sacrifices involved,' Clay said.

'You didn't have to give up your work.'

'Are you fighting?' Nicky looked from one to the other.

The anxious look in the child's eyes overrode Dallas's irritation with Clay. 'No, darling. We're having a discussion, but the dinner table isn't the place for it. Did you tell Clay what you've decided to name the calf?'

'Teddy,' Nicky said immediately. 'Because he looks like a teddy bear.' She slanted her eyes up at Clay. 'Are you going to yell at Dallas?'

Dull colour appeared on Clay's cheeks. 'Of course not.'

'I thought you weren't going to yell,' Dallas said later as Clay glowered at her from in front of the fireplace.

'I'm not yelling. I'm merely pointing out my objections to your going to work.'

'At least you might wait until you hear what my plans are before you object.'

'My wife doesn't need to work.' Clay's arms were folded across his chest, his long legs spread apart. His whole body-language shouted inflexibility.

'Is that your opinion or mine?' Dallas asked. 'If your male ego is worried that someone might think you can't support me, you'll be happy to know that I'll be volunteering my services.' She took a deep breath and tried reason. 'Sara doesn't need my help here, and I feel I'm needed at the school.'

Her words failed to take the chill off his manner. 'Nicky needs you, too. That's why you're here, or have you forgotten?'

'No, I haven't forgotten. I'll only be going in two or three times a week. I'll ride in with Nicky and come home when she does.' She could be as stubborn as he was. 'I wasn't aware that I needed to ask permission every time I breathed.' She faced him defiantly. 'I've already made arrangements with the elementary school principal.'

'I see.' Clay turned and jabbed at the embers in the fireplace. Sparks flew into the air. 'I guess I was naïve to expect you to discuss something like this with me before you made a decision.' Laying down the poker, he started from the room.

'What would you have said if I had discussed it with you?'

'I guess we'll never know, will we?'

Dallas wasn't surprised when Clay left her strictly alone that night; it was exactly what she would have expected of him. He probably thought he was punishing her by not gracing her bed with his exalted presence. As if she'd wanted to share her bed with a man who was suffering from an overdeveloped, old-fashioned sense of macho posturing. Me Tarzan, king of the jungle, you Jane, the little woman. He was probably pouting because he wanted her available to follow him around and exclaim how wonderful he was and to feel his muscles. She punched her pillow. The last thing she wanted to think about was Clay's muscles.

Much better to think of his selfish, unreasonable attitude. She'd been leading her own life for years, she argued to herself. It had never occurred to her that she should consult Clay about working at the school for a few hours a week. She was a grown woman—she didn't need his permission. Clay should trust her. Did he really think she'd be selfish enough to do something that might harm Nicky? All right, so maybe she shouldn't have committed herself without consulting him first, but there was no reason in the world for her to feel as if she'd hurt his feelings. Even if she had acted precipitately, he'd acted like a left-over from the nineteenth century.

After a sleepless night, Dallas was ready to meet Clay halfway in reconciling their differences. If he was ready to behave rationally, she'd promise to discuss any major decisions with him in the future. The problem was how to approach him. Dallas decided she'd go out and help him feed the cattle. Surely he would understand the significance of such a move.

Clay was saddling a large brown horse down by the corral. He flicked a glance in her direction, taking in her warm clothing, but said nothing.

'I thought maybe I could come along,' Dallas said.

'I'm not taking the truck today. I'm riding.'

Dallas reached up and stroked the horse's nose. 'Do you have a horse I could ride?'

Clay paused, his hands resting on his horse. Finally he said, 'Go ask Sara for some boots. I'll saddle Molly for you.'

Molly was yellow and big as a barn. 'You don't really expect me to ride this monster, do you?' Dallas asked, eyeing the horse doubtfully.

Clay gave her a mocking look. 'Changing your mind?'

'No. I'll manage.' The mare stood still as a statue while Dallas scrambled awkwardly into the saddle. Molly was as wide as she was tall. 'I feel as if I'm doing the splits,' Dallas moaned as Clay adjusted her stirrups.

'Molly's mostly buckskin, but I suspect she has some draught horse in her. More importantly, her heart and patience are as large as she is.' He vaulted into his saddle with enviable ease.

Dallas followed Clay's brown horse from the corral, hesitant to bring up their argument. 'Where are we going?'

'When Jim went out to feed yesterday, he thought there were a few cows missing,' Clay said. 'He and Loren checked out what they could by pick-up, but there's a few draws they couldn't get to. We'll have to search them by horse.'

'You mean there could be more freezing calves down there?'

'Or a cow could get its foot caught in some fence wire.' He indicated the pliers hanging from his saddle. 'There's lots of possibilities.'

'I always thought of farming and ranching as summer occupations with nothing much happening in the winter.'

'This is one of our busiest seasons,' Clay said. 'Not only do we have to feed the cows, but calving time can have us working twenty-four hours a day. After calving comes breeding. Then, in the summer, we lease land in the mountains and move the cattle up there. Plus there's the haying to do. Come fall we have to bring the cattle back home, and there's the weaning and shipping to market. In our spare time we fight poisonous weeds in the pastures, fix fences, repair broken-down machinery and doctor sick cows. And then there's the record-keeping. Ranching is like any other business—lots of paperwork.'

'Which all seems to fall on you.'

Clay nudged his horse along. 'Dad sort of lost heart after Mom died. He kept at it until I could take over, but now he's happiest with his other interests. He still owns half the ranch and helps out now and again. Even though I only own a quarter and a quarter is in trust for Nicky, I manage the whole parcel.'

'You really enjoy it, don't you?'

Clay reined his horse to a stop. One hand resting on his thigh, he waved the other in a wide circle. 'Look around you. The Spanish Peaks, the Culebras, the Sangre de Cristos, Mount Mestas, Silver Mountain... beautiful, aren't they? The breezes sweeping down them are filled with stories of fabulous gold mines and legendary travellers. Aztec legend says the Spanish Peaks used to be an earthly paradise before men angered the rain god who then made this valley like the rest of the earth.' Looking down, he said. 'These high grasslands might not look much like paradise, but grama grass and buckhorn cholla have their own beauty. And over there.' Shading his eyes, he pointed off in the distance at a small herd of brown and white animals. 'You won't see those on Capital Hill. Pronghorn antelope.'

'It's more than just a way for you to make money, isn't it?'

Clay leaned back in his saddle. 'Ranching isn't fancy hats and hand-tooled leather boots. It's dirt and sweat and heat and cold. Money's nice to have, but beauty, freedom, the satisfaction of a job well done, those are the things that count in life, no matter what a man does.'

'I feel as passionate about what I do. And I'm needed at the school,' Dallas said.

Clay flicked his reins, heading his horse down into a draw.

She should have known this wouldn't be easy. Why couldn't she just admit to Clay that she was partly in the wrong? Just because he was stubborn, it didn't mean she had to be. On the other hand, she refused to have Clay thinking he could run her life. Dallas studied his back as she followed him down the incline. The air was crisp, and Clay's goosedown jacket emphasised his broad shoulders. Nice shoulders. Strong and sinewy, with muscles that flexed under one's palms. Suddenly Molly lurched to her knees, and Dallas flew forward over the horse's neck, the saddle-horn jamming hard into her stomach. Before Dallas could even cry out, they were at the bottom of the draw and Molly had righted herself.

Clay was out of his saddle, his hands deftly inspecting Molly's front legs. 'You OK?' he asked without looking up.

'Six broken ribs, but don't let that bother you,' Dallas answered sweetly. 'As long as Molly's OK, that's what counts.'

Clay finished inspecting Molly's legs and pulled his glove back on before answering. 'I can't find any damage. She came down too fast and slipped on that patch of ice. Didn't you see it?'

'No, I——'.

'A horse breaks a leg, there's not much we can do.' Clay was holding Molly's bridle, patting her neck. He didn't look at Dallas. 'If she'd sprained something, one of us might have had to walk back.'

'And I can guess which one.'

Clay squinted up at her. 'Claiming special privileges because you're a woman?'

'Certainly not. I——'

'I'll ask you again.' He might not have heard her denial. 'Are you OK?'

'Yes.' She practically spit the word at him.

'We can always turn back.'

'I said I'm fine.'

Clay shrugged and remounted, the saddle creaking beneath his weight as he settled into it. The horses snorted in the cold air and the snow crunched beneath their hoofs. Clay led the way up one draw and down another while Dallas glared at his back. The near accident had been all his fault. He could have mentioned the ice. Even if she'd seen it, how was she supposed to know that horses could slip on ice? Besides, he was the one distracting her. 'Daydreaming?' She could almost hear her father's voice. 'That's how accidents happen.'

Ahead of her, Clay stood up in his stirrups and studied the surrounding area and then headed up a faint trail out of the draw. Dallas followed miserably behind. She'd acted like a spoiled brat, demanding that Clay be more concerned about her than her horse. She leaned over and patted Molly on the neck. 'I'm really glad you're all right,' she said softly to the horse. Molly flicked her ears in response.

'Loosen up on the reins and give her her head,' Clay said from the rim of the draw. 'She'll find her own footing coming up.' When Dallas had completed the journey up without incident, Clay turned his horse. 'We'll head back now.'

Dallas wanted to protest. All the draws had been empty. She opened her mouth to ask Clay where the cows were, but her words dried up at the sight of the unyielding back ahead of her.

Back at the corral, Dallas rushed to dismount, determined to prove to Clay that she could do something right. Her muscles were stiff from the unaccustomed activity. Painfully tossing her right leg over the back of the saddle, she dropped to the ground. Unfortunately she had forgotten how tall Molly was and how far off the ground her stirrups were. Her right foot frantically seeking the ground, her left foot barely in the stirrup, Dallas lost her balance and plummeted to earth, landing flat on her back.

'Are you all right?' Clay ducked quickly under his horse's neck.

'Yes.'

'You're sure?' He went down on one knee. 'Nothing broken?'

'I said I'm OK, didn't I?' Embarrassment gave a sharp edge to her words. 'I always get off a horse this way. I was merely tired and felt like lying down.' Her glare dared him to dispute her.

Clay sat back on his haunches, approval in his eyes, a grin on his face. 'Why should you be tired? Molly did all the work. All you did was sit there. What a tenderfoot you are.'

Dallas rubbed her backside ruefully. 'It's not my feet that are tender. I may never sit down again. Especially on a moving barrel. I never used to get sore—I must be getting soft.'

'There's nothing wrong with a soft woman.' Standing, Clay reached down and pulled her to her feet. 'Where are you sore?'

'Everywhere.' The teasing lights in his eyes gave her courage. Concentrating on the top of his zipper, she said, 'Clay, I'm sorry about yesterday. I should have consulted you before I committed myself. And I'm sorry about what happened earlier... when Molly almost fell. You were right to be concerned about her, and I was wrong to be so snotty about it.'

Clay tipped up her chin. 'I didn't behave so well last night myself. I should know that you'd weigh all the factors before you made a decision, and you'd never do anything that would harm Nicky.' His gloved thumb caressed her cheek. 'As for out there, a man's wife should come before his horse.'

Dallas couldn't tear her gaze from his. 'No...no, you were...' Words caught in her throat as Clay's eyes darkened to deep indigo. Suddenly an unexpected shove between her shoulder-blades sent her careening into Clay's arms.

He laughed as his arms tightened about her waist, pulling her hips to rest against his. 'Apparently Molly takes exception to my remark.'

Dallas had forgotten that they were standing between the two horses. 'Every woman wants to come first with a man,' she said without thinking. Instantly she wished she could take the words back. Would Clay think she was referring to the two of them? Would he feel compelled to explain that someone else would always be first in his heart? She rushed to divert his thoughts. 'Molly is probably trying to remind us that she's still wearing her saddle while we're standing around gabbing.'

'Could be. Some women are so impatient.' His hands dropped down to rub her bottom. 'You're sure you're not hurt?'

Her breath caught in her throat as unexpected waves of desire flowed over her. 'I'll be all right.' She brought her hands up to push against his shoulders to free herself from his embrace. At least, that's what she intended. Instead she found her hands gliding up his chest to link behind his neck. 'I enjoyed the ride.'

Clay's eyes crinkled at the corners. 'You must be a glutton for punishment.' He switched from a hard massaging of her bottom to making slow circles around her hips. 'I enjoyed having you with me. Married life seems to agree with me. How about you?'

'I-I . . .' She could scarcely breathe. Clay's lips were so close to hers. If she raised her mouth just a little...the cold air, the pain and stiffness of her body, the smell of the horses, all fled before the intoxicating feel of Clay's lips on hers. Dallas stood on tiptoe, her arms clenched tightly around Clay's neck, as she strained to return his kiss. Impatient to feel his hair slide through her fingers, first she discarded her gloves, then pushed his hat from his head. His laughing protest parted his lips to her searching tongue. His mouth was warm and moist and then two gloved hands fastened on to her cheeks and held her mouth locked to his as Clay sought and captured her tongue with his own. The stiffening left Dallas's legs and she melted against Clay's body.

He lifted his head. One gloved thumb rubbed across her throbbing lower lip. 'What you need is a long, hot bath.'

The low, intimate tone of his voice sent flames licking deep within her stomach. 'Y-yes.' Desire swelled her breasts beneath her clothing at the sleepy-eyed look on Clay's face.

'I'll be happy to scrub your back.' His thumb slid from her lips and began to trace the line of her chin. The light touch was hypnotic and Dallas closed her eyes and raised her face again to his, her lips parting in unspoken invitation.

CHAPTER SIX

'HEY, Clay, you want I should take care of the horses?'

At the sound of Jim's voice, Clay's hands dropped heavily to Dallas's shoulders and he lifted his head. 'No.' He cleared his throat. 'I'll take care of them.' His eyes were expressionless as he looked down at Dallas. 'As I said. A hot bath.' He didn't repeat his offer of help.

'I should help with the horses,' she said.

Clay gathered up the reins. 'Go on up to the house.' His brusque tone of voice was a clear dismissal.

'I'll take care of Molly for you.' Jim didn't look at her as he patted the large horse.

Embarrassment flamed on Dallas's face. Clay's opinion of his wife was obvious to everyone. Pride came to her rescue. Just because Clay treated her as if she were a leper it didn't mean she couldn't behave with dignity. 'Thank you, Jim.' Her voice was cool and composed, proof that she didn't care one bit if her husband was an arrogant boor.

Jim gave her a smile that unmistakably apologised for her husband before he turned to Clay. 'Kim said to tell you that she got As on her maths and English exams.'

Sara had told Dallas that her and Jim's daughter was attending the university in Fort Collins, and Dallas added her congratulations to Clay's. 'You must be very proud of her.'

104

'We are. She's been wanting to be a veterinarian ever since she was knee-high to a grasshopper.' Jim didn't bother to disguise his pride. 'First one in my family to go to college. Thanks to Clay.'

'Why Clay?' Dallas asked.

'I thought you were going to go take a bath,' Clay said.

Dallas ignored him and waited for Jim's answer.

'Even with the scholarship Kim won, Sara and I just didn't see how we could swing the cost. But Clay's got a real thing about how important education is, and he said anyone who worked that hard deserved to go, so he's making up the difference.'

It was clear that Clay preferred not to discuss his generosity. Giving Jim a look of disgust, he said, 'You were right about the cattle. The count is short.'

Dallas had started for the house but now she turned to protest. 'Why did we quit looking if they weren't all there? Am I that bad a rider?'

'It had nothing to do with you,' Clay said impatiently. 'We quit looking because the cows aren't there.'

'But where could they be?' she asked.

'Well, they didn't grow wings and fly away.'

'You mean rustlers? I thought they went out with covered wagons,' Dallas said.

'They're still around,' Jim said. 'Only today they drive trucks. They steal a half-dozen or so cattle and are across the state line in a couple of hours.'

'It seems like a lot of trouble for six cows,' she said.

'Does several thousand dollars sound better?' Clay asked.

'For only six cows?' At his nod, she asked, 'Why don't you stop them?'

'When you come up with a sure-fire method of doing so, why don't you call up the Cattlemen's Association or the Colorado State Patrol. I'm sure they'll be happy to know there is one,' Clay said, every word overlaid with sarcasm. 'In the meantime, would you go soak in the tub? You can hardly walk. I shouldn't have taken you with me.'

Dallas spun angrily about. Everything she did reminded Clay that she didn't belong here. She was wearing overshoes for warmth on top of the borrowed boots and the unfamiliar footwear made her clumsy, causing her to stumble.

Clay was immediately at her side, grabbing her arm with a force that made it ache. 'For heaven's sake, can't you do anything?'

'No.' She'd say it before he did. 'Not here. Because I don't belong here.'

He dropped her arm. 'It's a little late to come to that conclusion, isn't it?'

A week later, Clay's words still rang in her ears as Dallas leaned forward, resting her right arm on the saddle-horn. 'Horses are lucky,' she said out loud. Molly gave a little hop at the unexpected sound of Dallas's voice, and Dallas reached down and patted the buckskin mare's neck. 'Stallions are stallions. But Clay... he's so complicated, he's driving me crazy. I guess he didn't approve of my kissing him in the barnyard. He hasn't been near me since.' Molly's ears twitched. 'Oh, sure. We eat dinner together. We even have civilised conversation. Politics, the weather, what's happening in the neighbourhood, my days at school, Colorado history.' She gave a half-hearted laugh. 'Sometimes Clay sounds like a one-man Colorado visitors' bureau. He loves this place. And who could blame him? So do I.' The difference was, Colorado was in Clay's blood. He belonged here.

Molly tugged at the reins, tired of standing. Dallas loosened her hold, giving the mare her head. Let Molly take her where she wanted—one trail was as good as another. Jim said she couldn't get lost, that Molly always knew the way home. Certainly the mare seemed to know where she was going as she picked her way up an unseen trail. Dallas had ridden every opportunity she had, determined to prove she wasn't a total flop at ranch living. Jim or Nicky normally rode with her. This was the first time she'd had enough confidence in her riding skills to venture out alone. Not that one needed much skill with Molly. The large horse was remarkably forgiving of the amateur rider on her back. Nicky said that Alanna had favoured Molly, too.

Lost in her thoughts, Dallas would have missed the cabin hidden in the clump of pines if Molly hadn't walked straight up to the small porch and halted by an old hitching-post. Dallas slid from the saddle. Molly pawed at the snow, uncovering some hay. Dallas laughed. 'You greedy old thing. How did you know that food was there? You must have the best nose in the west.' Tying Molly's reins loosely so that she could reach the hay, Dallas looked around.

Further back in the trees leaned a small shanty with a half-moon cut in the door. An outhouse. Behind Dallas, Molly made snuffling sounds as she ate. The faint cry of a crow floated down to earth as he rode the thermals. The cabin was quiet.

Dallas stepped cautiously up on the porch. Enormous logs had weathered over the years to a soft grey. The door was bolted on the outside. Dallas hesitated with her hand on the bolt. Someone had installed glass in the old window-frames, and she tiptoed over to one. The pane was dusty, and she rubbed clean an area large enough to look through.

The cabin was one room, spartan, yet cosy. Two bunks were built against one wall, the bottom one covered with a gaily striped blanket. Across the room was a small wooden table with two chrome and plastic kitchen chairs looking incongruous beside it. A blue metal coffee-pot sat on the hearth in front of the stone fireplace. In spite of the coffee-pot and the blanket, the cabin looked abandoned. From the window Dallas could see dust on the table and cobwebs hanging from the upper bunk. The temptation to go inside for a closer look was irresistible.

Inside the cabin, the air was stale and a few dead flies dotted the floor. Dallas was surprised to see a bookcase under the window she'd been peering in. She moved towards it. Adventure stories, animal stories and stories of the Old West were jammed into the small case along with tales of jet pilots, explorers and sports heroes. Dallas thumbed through the books. The same names were repeated on the fly leaves. Clay Dalton and Kyle Dalton. She smiled. Whatever this cabin had been built for, it had obviously served time as some sort of clubhouse for Clay and Kyle when they were younger. She picked up the books on the Old West. It was no surprise that they had been Clay's. Several looked interesting, and she decided to take them. Nicky might enjoy hearing them read. Pulling the books from the shelf disclosed a leather-bound book thrust behind. Dallas reached curiously for it.

The book was a diary. Alanna's name was embossed on the front in gold. Dallas had forgotten Alanna's habit of writing down all the important events in her life. She rubbed her hand over the cool leather, fighting the temptation to read Alanna's innermost thoughts. What Alanna had written about Clay was none of Dallas's business. On the other hand, what if Alanna had written of her hopes and aspirations for Nicky? As Nicky's surrogate mother, wasn't Dallas obligated to know? Besides, the diary was something that Nicky might appreciate in later years, a key to her mother. Dallas could never give the diary to Alanna's child without first ensuring that the diary contained nothing that would turn Nicky away from her mother.

'Here you are.'

Dallas whirled about, dropping the armload of books. Clay stood in the cabin doorway watching her with a quizzical look on his face. 'Guilty conscience?'

'No. Of course not. I just didn't hear you.' She bent down to pick up the books, sliding the diary between the others to hide it from Clay's view. 'What are you doing here?'

'I was worried. Jim said you rode off several hours ago.'

'I didn't realise that I'd been gone so long, but there was no need for you to worry,' Dallas said.

'Wasn't there?' One corner of Clay's face twisted in a wry smile. 'You forget I've seen you on a horse.'

'Just because I wasn't at my best that day——'

'We agree on something.' He ambled into the room and took the top book from her hand, reading the title on the spine. 'Something to help you sleep at night?'

His words reminded her of the night he'd offered himself to help her sleep, and she couldn't stop the heat that flushed her face. 'I was taking them back for Nicky. Do you mind?'

'No. Why should I?'

'They're yours,' Dallas said.

'I'd forgotten they were even here.'

'What is this place?'

'An old squatter's cabin.'

'What do you think happened to the people who lived here?'

Clay shrugged. 'Hard to say. I've always heard it was empty when Walt took over here.' He looked around. 'Indians could have scared them off, or a hard winter. They might have decided that gold-hunting was easier. Or maybe the man's wife was too soft for life out here so she just upped and left him and went back to her home in the east.'

Dallas's hands clenched around the books. No misinterpreting that job. She changed the subject. 'It made an ideal playhouse for you and Kyle. Did you come here often?'

'When we were younger. We'd pack supper and spend the night.' He shook his head impatiently as if ridding himself of old memories. 'That was a long time ago.'

'Who uses it now?' She nodded towards the blanketed bunk.

'No one.' Only the barest hint of some quickly suppressed emotion in Clay's eyes told her he was lying. He stretched out one hand. 'I'll carry those back for you.'

Dallas hastily stepped back out of his reach. 'No. That is, I can handle them. I brought a bag with an apple and a Thermos of water. It's hanging on the saddle-horn. I can put the books in that. After I give Molly the apple, that is.' She was babbling. 'You don't need to wait for me. Molly will find her way back. Jim said so.' Her voice dried up at the cynical look on Clay's face.

'Why do I get the impression you want to get rid of me?'

'Don't be ridiculous.' Her nose in the air, she sailed past him through the open doorway.

'I'd hate to think I barged in when you were expecting someone else.'

Dallas turned from feeding Molly the apple sections and stared at him as he shot the bolt in place. 'That's absurd. Who would I be meeting? Jim?' She giggled at the thought. 'Sara would rip his head off. And, in case you haven't heard, Loren only has eyes for that red-headed waitress at the café in town.'

Clay came around Molly and put one hand on the saddle-horn and one on the back of the saddle, pinning Dallas between him and the horse. 'And you, Mrs Dalton...who do you have eyes for?' He reached down and brushed a tendril of hair from her face.

Dallas swallowed hard at the seductive tone of Clay's voice. 'No one.' She pressed against Molly and the horse stamped her feet impatiently. 'We'd better go.'

'What's your hurry?'

'You said it yourself—I've been gone a long time. People will worry.'

Clay's eyes narrowed thoughtfully. 'You seem awfully anxious to get away from this cabin. Why is that?'

Dallas gave a loud sigh of exasperation and ducked under Clay's arm before he could stop her. At the cabin door, she turned and tapped her foot on the porch boards. 'All right. Open the door. We'll go inside and sit there until you're satisfied that I did not intend to meet any one here. I didn't even know this cabin was here.'

'Then how did you find it?' He rested his forearms on Molly's saddle and spoke to Dallas over the mare's back.

'I didn't find it. Molly did. I suppose she smelled the hay buried under the snow there. Anyway, she walked right up to it.' Clay continued to stare in her direction, but Dallas had the feeling that he wasn't seeing her.

Finally he gave a slight nod. Untying Molly's reins, he led her forward. 'Come on. Let's get back. It's almost time for you to meet the school bus.'

Dallas made no move to do his bidding. She stood with her fists braced on her hips. 'That's it? No apology for making ridiculous accusations?'

Clay pushed his hat to the back of his head. 'You know what, Dallas? You drive me crazy.'

Before she could grasp his intention, he jumped up on the porch and swept her into his arms. 'Put me down,' she ordered.

Molly was standing beside the porch, and Clay dumped Dallas into the saddle. The unceremonious action startled Dallas and she would have fallen from the horse if Clay hadn't steadied her. 'I can see how much your riding has improved,' he said.

Dallas ignored his mocking words, giving Molly a nudge. The horse obediently started off. The ride back to the ranch was accomplished in silence. Dallas was determined to prove to Clay that she wasn't a total failure on a horse. At the corral she successfully dismounted and turned to Clay. He was still astride his horse, the afternoon sun silhouetting his head and preventing her from seeing his face. 'Well?' she demanded, waiting for an acknowledgement of her improved skills.

'What did you take from the cabin?'

Dallas gasped. 'Books. You said it was OK.'

'Besides the books. What was it you didn't want me to see?'

She started to deny his accusations and then changed her mind. Flinging her head up, she stared at him defiantly. 'Alanna's diary.'

'I thought it must be something like that, as skittish as you were.' Dismounting, he lifted the bag from her saddle.

'Give it back,' Dallas said, reaching out with her hand.

Clay dug into the bag and pulled out the leather-bound book. 'I didn't know Alanna kept a diary.'

'Not every night. She wrote down things important to her.'

Clay turned the book over in his hands, a frown wrinkling his brow. 'I hope you're not planning on reading this,' he finally said. 'It would be a mistake. Leave the past alone.'

'There might be things in there I should know. About Nicky.' She eyed him defiantly, knowing he'd see through the fragile cloak of deception she'd woven to cover her intent.

Clay's eyes filled with a resignation tinged with sadness. 'Whatever Alanna needed, was looking for, it doesn't matter now. She's at peace. Let her stay that way.'

She knew Clay was right, but she was driven by an inner compulsion to know the truth. 'I would never do anything that hurt Alanna.'

'Are you sure the reverse is true?' Clay draped the bag over her outstretched arm. With a sigh, he brushed his hand across her cheek. 'I hate to see you get hurt.'

Hours later Dallas threw the diary across the room. If Clay didn't want to see her hurt, he shouldn't have returned it to her. No, she couldn't blame Clay. He hadn't been the least bit fooled by her lame excuse that she needed to read it for Nicky's sake. He'd tried to dissuade her, but a runaway freight train would have been easier to stop. And now her stubborn perversity had received its unwelcome reward. The diary provided startling confirmation that Clay and Alanna had been lovers. Dallas blinked away hot tears. What a fool she was. She could no longer deceive herself. In spite of all evidence to the contrary, she'd hoped that the diary would prove that Clay and Alanna meant nothing to each other. Instead....Alanna's words were inscribed on Dallas's mind with indelible ink.

'I know Kyle is having an affair with that woman,' Alanna had written. 'But I'll not give him the satisfaction of finding out I know. I'll show him that he can't put me aside as if I were nobody.' Later she'd planned her revenge. 'There is no one I could take for a lover who would anger and upset Kyle more. What's more, I swear he's willing although he's said nothing. It will be up to me to prod him along.' An entry made weeks later proved that the man had, indeed, been willing. 'I started this affair for revenge,' read Alanna's words. 'How diverting to discover that I'm beginning to care for this man. Maybe because he's so obviously in love with me. Such devotion disarms me. Even to you, dear diary, I won't name him. But I must call him something. D.P. Yes, dearest D.P. Kyle would be furious if he found out. Once I wanted him to discover us. I dreamt of being naked in my lover's arms and Kyle charging into the cabin. No longer. I must think of D.P. Kyle would destroy him and take Nicky from me. I can't risk that. I must have both Nicky and D.P. I can hear him coming now, and I know that his dark blue eyes will be burning with passion for me.'

Dallas read no further. At first the initials D.P. had confused her. Alanna couldn't mean Clay. Then she'd realised that Alanna wouldn't have given the man's true initials. And with that realisation had come the truth. D.P. Alanna's code was pathetically simple. She'd merely reversed the initials. D.P. was really P.D. There were two P.D.s on the Dalton ranch. One was Peter Dalton, the father of Clay and Kyle. Dallas had considered him momentarily, but Peter's eyes were a faded blue. Alanna would never have written that Peter's eyes were dark blue with passion. That left one other. In her mind's eye Dallas could see Clay signing their marriage certificate: Clay Peter Dalton. Named for his father. Clay with dark blue eyes. Eyes that Dallas had seen burning with passion. For her. As a substitute for his dead lover.

No wonder Clay had warned her against reading the diary. The cabin had been his and Alanna's love-nest. Alanna must have ridden Molly there numerous times. Molly hadn't smelled the hay—she'd remembered it. And Clay... Accusing her of arranging to meet someone there had been his own conscience acting up.

If a conscience he had. Pacing the length of the room, Dallas kicked the diary angrily, and it skittered beneath her bed. Let it lie there. She had no desire to read any further. Once she'd wished that Clay would admit his relationship with Alanna. How naïve to believe that knowing he'd loved Alanna would bring them closer. What kind of man made love to his brother's wife? The thought of such a man making love to her made her feel unclean. And betrayed.

'Still up?'

Dallas froze. Striving to bring her heaving emotions under control, she slowly turned. Clay was in her doorway, leaning against the door-jamb, the casual pose belied by the intensity with which he studied her face. 'I read the diary,' she said.

'So I see. I warned you.'

She drew a ragged breath. 'Why didn't you get rid of it?'

'I would have if I'd known about it.' He jammed his hands into his pockets. 'I suppose she wrote down everything.'

Dallas could barely nod her head. How could he sound so unconcerned?

'I'm sorry,' Clay said. 'I thought it better if you didn't find out.' He straightened up and walked into the room, eyeing her warily. One hand reached out and wiped moisture from her cheek. 'I know you're upset. Would you like me to stay?'

Dallas jerked her head away. 'Don't touch me.'

Clay's body went still. 'I see. Alanna mentioned me.'

Dallas turned away, her throat clogged with tears. 'Did you truly expect her not to?'

'No. I guess not.' He paused in the open doorway. 'I suggest you burn that damned diary.'

'Burning it changes nothing.'

'I know you need some time to deal with this, Dallas. But think about a couple of things. The past is over. Our marriage isn't.' He paused. 'Unless you want it to be?'

'Do you?' she cried.

'Nothing has changed as far as I'm concerned. Nicky still needs to be part of a loving family. I think I can give her that. Can you?' He walked out of the room.

His words had been almost an accusation, as if she were the guilty party. Dallas glared at the empty doorway. How could she simply forget the whole affair? If only she'd listened to Clay and not read the diary. In time she could have convinced herself that Clay wouldn't have carried on an affair with his brother's wife right under Kyle's nose.

She paced the length of her bedroom floor. She thought she had known her cousin, and yet the diary proved that Alanna had set out to ensnare Clay for her own nefarious purposes. Alanna had had such a need to be loved. The discovery that her husband had supplanted her with another must have devastated her. Dallas threw herself on to her bed. Why hadn't Alanna just left Kyle? Why drag Clay into her web of deceit? Alanna had been a beautiful, desirable woman. No man could have resisted her siren song of loveliness. No, that wasn't true. A man with integrity would have resisted. Dallas wiped away the tears streaming down her face with an impatient hand. She couldn't excuse Clay.

But that wasn't the issue. Could she stay married to him? Lying on the bed, she clenched her fists at her sides. Impossible. She'd tell Clay... Suddenly his last words hit her like a ton of bricks. Nicky needed them. Both of them. Dallas rolled over and buried her face in her pillows. Clay was right—nothing had changed. She had married Clay to provide Nicky with a loving home. No promises had been made that she and Clay would ever share more than a concern for the child. Only her foolishness had led her to hope that time would bring, if not love, at least mutual respect.

Sitting up, Dallas wiped away her tears. For the last time. No longer would she cry for the cousin who'd deceived her. No longer would she cry over a marriage that represented nothing more than obligation and responsibility. She loved Nicky. She'd continue with the marriage for her sake. As for Clay...she swallowed hard. She'd uphold her end of the bargain. Maybe in time the sense of betrayal would ease.

Clay's prompt response to her knock proved that he was also unable to sleep. A strange light flared in his eyes, and Dallas tightened the belt of her chenille robe. His eyes turned opaque. 'I take it you've reached a decision,' he said.

'I'm staying, but...' Clay was standing too close. He'd shaved before dinner and the scent of his aftershave still perfumed the air. His terry robe was loosely belted, exposing his chest. To put some distance between them, she walked into the room. A mistake. The covers on Clay's bed were thrown back, invitingly, as if he'd been lying there.

'But?'

She spun about at Clay's question. For a moment she was unable to comprehend his meaning and then, with sheer will-power, she gathered her scattered thoughts. 'I-I would prefer that we—we didn't...for a while...'

Clay closed the space between them. Holding her chin up for his scrutiny, he said, 'I take it a cessation of marital relations is to be my punishment.'

Her skin burned beneath his touch. 'No. That is...not forever. I just need a little time.' Dallas was disgusted to realise that it sounded as if she was pleading with him, and she hardened her voice. 'Considering everything, I don't think I'm asking so much. But maybe asking you to be celibate for a short period of time is beyond your capabilities.'

Clay dropped his hand as if she'd burned him. 'You've made your point.' Turning from her, he walked over to the end of his bed. 'When do you think you'll let me out of the dog-house?'

'How dare you make a mockery of this?'

'Damn it, Dallas, I don't need you to tell me how I ought to feel.' His knuckles were white as he clenched the bedpost. 'If I live to be one hundred, I'll never forget the look on Kyle's face when he walked in and saw us.'

'Kyle saw you?' Dallas gasped in horror.

'Yes. I tried to explain, but he brushed me off. That was the night of the accident. I never had a chance to set the record straight with him.'

'You think you could? Alanna was his wife!'

'And you're mine.' Clay turned to face her. 'Apparently your marriage vows mean nothing to you.'

The irony of his accusation left her momentarily speechless. 'You're despicable!' she finally choked out.

Clay grabbed her arm, halting her flight from his room. 'I'll leave you alone for the present because I know the diary has upset you.'

'Upset!'

'But I warn you,' his hand tightened, 'don't try my patience too far.'

Dallas tried to jerk loose of his grasp—in vain. Clay meant her to know that he was in control. She ceased struggling and stared daggers at him. 'And if I do?'

His smile was not pleasant. 'I don't really think that's a problem, do you?'

'What does that mean?'

Clay gripped her other arm, forcing her to stand directly in front of him. 'It means, dear wife, that I'm well aware that banning me from your bed punishes you as much as me.'

'Hardly.'

'Liar.'

The soft-spoken word failed to warn Dallas of Clay's intentions. He yanked her up against his chest, his mouth swallowing her cry of outrage. She beat at his chest with her fists, but iron bands, one around her shoulders, one around her waist, held her captive. Suddenly her flailing hands struck warm skin. Her struggles had further parted Clay's robe. The temptation to flatten her palms and slide them over his skin was her undoing. His heart thudded wildly beneath her touch and her resistance ebbed.

Immediately Clay's lips, which had been forceful and demanding, softened. Little kisses, like tiny suction cups, pulled at the surface of her lips as Clay teased the perimeters of her mouth before blazing a fiery trail along her jawbone to beneath her ear. Dallas could no longer think, only feel, as he nibbled on her sensitive ear-lobe and then outlined the contours of her ear with his warm, moist tongue. Blood pulsed thunderously in her ears and ran riot through her veins, driving heat and desire before it. Her breasts swelled with need, and she swept aside the edges of Clay's robe and encircled his bare back with her hands, pressing her chest up against the strength of his. He'd found his way inside her robe and her flannel gown proved a flimsy barrier between her skin and his warm, stroking hands. His lips recaptured hers, and she met his thrusting tongue with fevered haste.

Clay lifted his head and slowly withdrew his hands from her robe, brushing his flat palms against the taut tips of her breasts. His touch elicited an involuntary gasp of pleasure from Dallas. He dropped his hands, a self-satisfied expression on his face. 'You may not like me, but you sure as hell desire me.'

His arrogant taunt stiffened her spine. 'All right. I admit that you are very adept at arousing and satisfying my physical urges.' She paused in his doorway for her parting shot. 'Does that gratify you? To know that a woman cares nothing about your mind, your personality, your soul—that all she's interested in is your body? That puts you on about the same level as an attractive toy.'

It said something for Clay's self-control that she was still alive, Dallas conceded several days later as she scraped old wallpaper from the dining-room walls. If the look on his face had been any indication, nothing would have given him greater pleasure than strangling her. She'd meant to anger him. Anything to shatter his gloating attitude and wipe the smirk from his face. The memory gave angry impetus to her movements. It would have been useless to deny that he'd affected her. He wasn't stupid. She only hoped his night had been as sleepless and tormented as hers.

Her arms ached and she leaned on the top rung of the ladder to rest a moment. Her marriage was either a tragedy or a farce. Since their angry words, she and Clay had maintained an unspoken, wary truce around each other. Judging by the raised eyebrows and cautious comments, they were deceiving no one on the ranch. Except Nicky. Nicky, at least, was content and secure in their love. And surely that was what mattered.

With a sigh, Dallas straightened up and attacked the wall once more. One advantage of a succession of Mrs Daltons all afraid to disturb the family shrine was that only one layer of paper had to be removed

before hanging the new paper. Yesterday her furniture had arrived and been partially distributed
through the house. A week ago that action would have
cheered her. Today it hardly mattered. New paint and
pretty wallpaper didn't make a home. Only love could
make a home.

'The way you're going at that wall I can't decide if
you're trying to remove wallpaper or tunnel your way
out.'

The unexpected comment startled Dallas and she
clutched at the ladder to steady herself. 'Must you
sneak up on me?'

Clay strolled into the room. 'You sure are making
a mess. Do you have any idea what you're doing?'

'I'm overwhelmed by your confidence in me.'

'You do have a tendency to tackle jobs that are
beyond your capabilities,' Clay said.

Dallas carefully wiped some debris from her scraper.
'Should I assume you are referring to our marriage?'

'Assume whatever you want. You will anyway.' Clay
picked up a roll of wallpaper from the dining-room
table. 'This what you're going to use in here? I like
it.'

His approval failed to appease her. 'Could I have
understood you correctly? One of my humble efforts
actually has your blessing? I'm overwhelmed. I must
mark this on the calendar. Today I actually did something right.'

'You've got barbed wire for a tongue.'

'Is that so?' Descending the ladder, she picked it
up to move it. 'I could have sworn there were times
when you found my tongue quite—unobjectionable.'

Clay took the ladder from her grasp and set it down
where she indicated. 'Are you trying to start
something?'

She climbed back up the ladder. 'Like what?'

. He leaned his hips against the dining-room table and crossed his arms in front of his chest. 'A fight that might end with me dragging you off that ladder.'

She gave him a look of disdain from her lofty perch. 'I thought we were having a civilised discussion, but maybe that's beyond your capabilities.' Angrily she slopped water on the wall to loosen the paper. 'If you think I'm trying to incite you to violence, you couldn't be more wrong.'

Clay raised a mocking brow. 'Who said anything about violence? You know damned good and well where it would end if I pulled you off that ladder.'

The truth of Clay's statement was irrefutable. They both realised that taking her in his arms destroyed her will to fight him. 'I'm not going to bother to deny the implications of your statement and give you an excuse to prove something we already know. I admit that I don't mind kissing you, but——'

'Don't mind?'

Dallas took a deep breath and ignored his mocking interjection. 'But that's beside the point. I——'

'What the hell is the point?' Clay grabbed both legs of the step-ladder and scowled up at her. 'That I haven't done enough penance or shown the proper amount of contrition?' He gave the ladder a slight shake for emphasis. 'How long do you intend to carry on this ridiculous holier-than-thou act? I never promised you that this marriage would be a walk in the park. At the first sign of trouble——'

'Hardly the first . . .'

'The first sign of trouble,' he repeated adamantly, 'you're ready to bail out.'

'I'm not bailing out. I——'

'What do you call it? I didn't marry you to have someone to repaper my dining-room.'

'No. You married me to take care of your niece. And I'm doing that.' Her chest was heaving with rage.

'I also told you that I wanted a real marriage.'

'And I told you I need more time.' She was gripping the ladder so tightly her hands hurt.

'How much time? Two weeks, two months, two years? How much time is enough to forget a past that has nothing to do with you? Why don't you admit it, Dallas? This isn't over something you read in Alanna's diary. That's only an excuse. You've spent your life flitting all over the world and now you don't want to settle down with a husband out here because you think it's the middle of nowhere. Only you're afraid to admit it, so you think you can drive me to ask you for a divorce. Well you can just forget all your hopeful schemes. I told you in the beginning that this marriage is for keeps.'

Dallas stared at him in disbelief. 'You're accusing me . . . ?'

'Prove me wrong. Welcome me to your bed tonight.'

His challenge was intolerable. At the same time, the image it conjured up sent a wave of heated desire through Dallas's body. To disguise her reaction, she sought refuge in scorn. 'You're incredible. You're the one who—who . . . and you have the audacity to twist things around to make it seem as if I'm the guilty party. It wasn't me Kyle was mad at when he died.'

Clay's head snapped back as if she'd slapped him. 'It must be very satisfying to be perfect.' His face was white to his lips. 'I'm sorry I bothered you. I'll let you get back to your work.' His hands dropped from the ladder and he turned away.

Immediately Dallas regretted her hateful remark. 'Clay, I'm sorry, I didn't mean...'

Clay's back was rigid as he paused in the doorway. 'Didn't mean what? That my brother was unforgivably hurt? That I will carry to the grave the look of betrayal on his face?'

'No. I...I'm just sorry.'

'Sorry that I killed my brother as surely as if I held a gun to his head because he was angry at me that night and drinking too much to forget what he thought I'd done?'

Dallas couldn't stand the pain in Clay's voice. 'No!'

'Never mind. I know why you're sorry. You're sorry you married me.'

CHAPTER SEVEN

'CLAY, wait.' Dallas jumped from the ladder. Haste made her careless, and she caught her toe on the bottom rung, collapsing the ladder and sending herself flying to the floor, her tools and the bucket of water crashing down beside her.

Clay was immediately at her side, swearing as he untangled the ladder from her arms and legs. 'You are the clumsiest...'

The anxious light in his eyes contradicted the angry snarling, and Dallas gave him a wan smile of reassurance. 'I always get off a ladder this way.'

'When you're tired.' He leaned the ladder against the wall.

Dallas nodded, pleased that the bleak look on Clay's face had faded slightly. She was wearing an old flannel shirt over her T-shirt, and she took it off and began mopping up the spilled water. What Clay had done couldn't be erased, and only an idiot would tell him he had no reason to feel guilty. They simply had to learn to live with his past, both of them—Dallas took a deep breath—starting now. 'Recriminations and angry words will get us nowhere,' she said, concentrating on finding all the spilled water. 'Maybe we can't wipe the slate clean, but at least we can turn the page.'

Clay dropped to the floor beside her and took the shirt from her hand. 'I'm willing to try if you are.' He squeezed the water from the fabric and draped it over the bucket. The blue of his eyes deepened as he pulled Dallas up to her knees. 'I've missed having a wife.'

His voice was a whisper of breath against her cheek before his mouth cut off any response. Her legs burned where his thighs touched hers. When his lips abandoned her mouth to burn a trail down her neck, she asked, 'Any wife?'

His chuckle tickled her skin. 'Not any wife. A stubborn, opinionated, bad-tempered wife with hazel eyes that spit sparks.' His mouth returned to hers, and he lightly bit the tip of her tongue. 'And with a barbed-wire tongue that I find quite—unobjectionable.'

She felt herself blush as he mimicked her earlier words. 'I don't exactly sound like the wife of a man's dreams.'

His tongue traced the curve of her ear. 'Who wants a dream wife?' Wrapping his arms around her, he buried his head in the crook of her neck. 'I prefer flesh and blood.' Pulling her with him, he sat back against the wall. 'What's this?' Reaching behind him, he pulled out a picture. 'The Witch of the Spanish Peaks. Where did you find her?'

Her emotions in turmoil, Dallas welcomed the respite that answering the question would give her. Reason indicated that inviting Clay back into her bed would be the quickest way to banish the spectre of the past, but deep within her was a tiny kernel of reluctance that, even as she failed to understand it, she could not ignore. 'I found her in the attic. She goes well with the wallpaper.' She frowned. 'But if she's a witch...'

'Not a real witch. She's an early ancestor. On my mother's side.' He rumbled with laughter. 'Kyle named her. The Spanish name for the Spanish Peaks is

Huajatolla, a corruption of the original Indian name, which meant "breasts of the world". You'll notice the lady of the portrait is well-endowed.' He held the picture out in front of them.

'That's your definition of a witch?'

'She also has a face that would stop a train. Little boys believe that witches are old crones.' He set the picture aside and turned to her. 'It isn't until they grow up and become bewitched that they learn the truth.'

Her eyes flickered shut beneath the intensity of his gaze. 'What truth?' she managed before he pulled her on to his lap facing him. His mouth came down on hers, demanding a response. Every nerve in her body was tingling by the time he lifted his head to answer her question.

'That it's women like you who are dangerous,' he said, cupping her face with his hands. He ran a thumb across her quivering lips. 'A mouth so soft and inviting should be outlawed.' His head descended, and her body trembled as he lightly ran his fingers down the front of her T-shirt.

By the time he released her lips, she knew what she had to do. Casting aside her doubts, she concentrated on a dark hank of hair that brushed the top of his collar. 'If you want to . . . that is . . . my bedroom door is open.'

Clay shook his head. 'As much as I want to accept . . .' Taking her hands from around his neck, he held them firmly against his chest. 'I'm not trying to seduce you into changing your mind.' He pressed a kiss into the palm of each hand. 'I can wait until you're sure.' He rose to his feet.

Dallas's eyes rose the long length of jean-clad legs, past the flannel-covered breadth of his chest to dark eyes which locked with hers. Her breath caught in her throat at the expression in Clay's eyes. To break the spell, she deliberately fluttered her lashes. 'Can you?' Her voice was rife with provocation.

'You are a witch.' Clay's voice was thick as he pulled her to her feet with one swift movement. 'Behave yourself or I'll forget why I came in here in the first place.' He dropped a quick, hard kiss on her lips. A kiss that held promise for the future. 'We're invited to a big shindig up in Colorado Springs on Saturday night. The Anderson's fiftieth wedding anniversary. They ranched north of here before retiring in the Springs. Most of the people you met the other night will be there. Along with about half of Colorado, if I know the Andersons. We'll fly up and spend the night.'

'I can't leave Nicky overnight,' Dallas said in dismay.

'Of course you can. Dad will come over and stay with her, and Sara will be close by.'

Dallas shook her head. 'No. It's too soon.'

'And when won't it be? Are we going to be confined to the ranch the rest of our lives because Nicky is afraid we won't come back? You're the one who keeps saying the longer we give in to her fears, the longer it will take her to conquer them.'

'I know.' She sank to her knees and aimlessly moved her tools around. 'She's doing so well. I don't want to rush things.'

'Be honest. You don't want to go because you don't like my friends.' He frowned down at her. 'Burt and Hazel Anderson stood up for my folks at their wedding. Going to their party would be too hard on Dad, so we're going as his representatives.'

'You go without me.' Taking her shirt from the bucket's rim, she carefully folded it up. Clay's stare was burning a hole in her. 'Tell everyone I'm sick or something. I'm not going.'

Clay gave a harsh laugh. 'I should have known your resolve to try harder was only empty words.'

His accusation cut deep, and she said, 'That's not fair. I meant with our marriage.'

'I'm asking you to go to a party with me. As my wife. To meet my friends. As much as you enjoy open bedroom doors, marriage is more than that.'

Dallas could feel her face flame. Clay went straight for the jugular vein. 'And I should have known that I couldn't count on you to understand.' She jumped to her feet, ignoring his outstretched hand. 'What time are we leaving on Saturday?'

Dallas could hear Clay in the adjoining hotel room as she fiddled with the honey-brown tendrils of hair that framed her face. Needlessly she checked the pins that secured her hair atop her head. She'd panicked when Clay had informed her that the party was formal, but they'd flown into Colorado Springs earlier in the day, and there had been plenty of time for her to shop for a dress while Clay had attended to some business.

She smoothed the salmon-coloured silk over her hips. Her heart was beating fast, sending waves of perfume into the air. Had she used too much scent? Her hand went to her throat and skin met skin. The real cause of her nervousness. What if Clay didn't like her dress? What if he thought it was too sophisticated, too provocative for a country-looking girl with freckled skin? She bent closer to the mirror. No amount of make-up could hide all those freckles. No wonder Clay could contain his desires. Separate hotel rooms.

'Knock, knock.' Clay breezed in without waiting for her reply. He held up his hands, his shirt cuffs flapping loosely at his wrists. 'I don't know what diabolical mind...' The sentence trailed off as he loosed a low whistle of admiration. 'Well, well, well, Mrs Dalton. I see you spent your afternoon profitably.'

'Like it?' She twirled for his approval. Anything to cover up the sudden desire that had surged through her body at his appearance. If Clay was tall and lean and masculine in his work clothes, in formal wear he was positively breathtaking. What was it about the solid white shirt front that made her crave to slide her palms up it?

Clay caught her hands and held them out from her sides as he studied her from head to toe. 'What happened to my wife? You know the lady I mean—the one in tight jeans and loose boots.'

She rescued her hands and, taking one of his cufflinks, inserted it in the cuff. Frowning over her task, she said, 'She lost her nerve, so sent me.' She risked a quick look upward. 'You don't mind?'

He held out his other arm. 'I'm not sure. Are you a witch, too?' His voice was low and seductive.

'Maybe.' Turning away, she picked up a comb and pretended to fix her hair.

Clay stood behind her, watching their twin images in the mirror. A hand around her midriff pulled her back against his lean body, enabling his fingers to trace the deep V of her neckline. 'You're tempting me, Mrs Dalton, to say the hell with my obligations.' He dropped a quick kiss on her shoulder and then moved away, only to stop in the doorway between their rooms. 'The Andersons have been like second parents to me, but right now I wish I'd never heard of them.'

In the hotel lift, Dallas gripped her purse tightly. The lift car was mirrored, reflecting back their images. She studied Clay in the mirror through her lashes. He wore his black formal wear with an easy elegance, but even the well-shaped jacket could not disguise the muscles that lay temporarily quiescent beneath the fabric. Her silk-clad arm barely touched him, but she could feel his hard strength, and each nervous breath she took was filled with his scent. She wanted to move away, but knew he'd correctly interpret such a move. The swift downward movement sent her stomach plunging.

'You'll be the belle of the ball,' Clay said.

'Being generous in your victory?'

Clay gave her a swift glance. 'I thought that military kids learned how to cope with life's changes and new experiences.' He moved aside as the doors silently opened.

Dallas stepped out. 'Some do and some drop out. I managed, but never silently. My mother used to beg me to quit verbally bleeding all over her.' She gave a half-laugh. 'I think I left my courage in the elevator.'

Clay stopped in the middle of the enormous lobby. 'You really are nervous about tonight,' he said slowly.

'Give the man an "A" for perception.'

'It never occurred to me...I thought you were being obstinate for the sheer pleasure of annoying me.'

Dallas half choked. 'You call me obstinate! You're the one getting your way. As usual, I might add.'

Clay guided her down the hall, bending his head to speak softly in her ear. 'That's funny. I can't remember the last time I had my own way... with you.'

The party was in full swing, music blasting through the double doors of the hotel ballroom. Taking Dallas's arm, Clay led her over to the receiving line and introduced her to the anniversary couple. After a few minutes of small talk, Dallas began to relax. Then, from across the room, she recognised the woman who'd made the poisonous remarks about Alanna. A craven impulse made her slip her hand into Clay's. He gave her fingers a comforting squeeze and guided her towards a bar set up in one corner. Glasses in hand, they rejoined the crowd that swirled about the edges of the dance-floor.

Several men hailed Clay, but he pointed towards the dance-floor. Dallas's conscience nipped at her, sure that Clay felt obliged to stay with her, having forced her to come. 'I feel like the proverbial ball and chain,' she said in a rush. 'You don't have to dance with me.'

Clay unleashed a slow, lazy smile at her. 'Aren't newly-weds supposed to be inseparable?'

Dallas caught her breath at the sensual gleam in Clay's eyes. The deep voice behind her was welcome.

'How the mighty have fallen.' A large, dark-haired man vigorously slapped Clay on his back as Dallas turned.

Vicky Gomez, Nicky's teacher, laughed as she watched the two men. 'Dallas, I want you to meet my husband Tony.'

His large hand swallowed Dallas's hand up. 'Vicky can't stop talking about all the great ideas you've given her. She was getting a little tired of teaching, but you've reinspired her.'

'All I did was——' Dallas started to say, self-consciously.

Vicky turned to Clay. 'All she did was totally rear-range my room so that I can manage my class better, not to mention giving me tips on discipline and how to communicate with the kids. I have one student that I'd absolutely despaired of. Her last teacher said she was a model child, but I found her totally incorrigible. It took Dallas to see that the poor kid was having trouble handling her folks' divorce. The kid still isn't a model student, but Dallas has been spending time with her and the progress is unbelievable. And just look at Nicky. Marrying Dallas is the best thing you could have done for your niece.' Vicky smiled at Dallas. 'Not that Clay married you for that reason, of course.'

Dallas smiled weakly back. 'Of course.'

Vicky turned back to Clay. 'When the principal at the high school heard about the classes Dallas presented back in Virginia teaching parents and teenagers how to communicate with each other, she immediately began making plans to borrow Dallas. I'll bet you never even considered what a godsend Dallas and her expertise would be to us all when you married her.'

'I can honestly say that didn't enter into my calculations. Maybe we should have discussed it,' Clay gave Vicky an engaging grin, 'but we always had other things to talk about.'

'I'll bet you did.' Vicky nudged her husband. 'Tony used to be romantic. Now all he talks about is stocks and bonds and mutual funds.' She rolled her eyes. 'Husbands.'

Husbands was a subject Vicky returned to several hours later as she sat in the lounge combing her hair while Dallas repaired her lipstick. 'You certainly caught the pick of the litter when you snagged Clay. Everyone from Denver south was green with envy. Even us old married hags. Tony and I went to school with Clay and Kyle. All the girls were wild about Clay.'

'What about Kyle?'

'Mercedes would have clawed out the eyes of any girl who looked at Kyle. Most of the girls preferred Clay, anyway, but he played the field. A date with him was like winning the lottery.'

'Does Tony know you have a crush on Clay?' Dallas teased.

'Tony's almost as bad. He was on the high school football team with Clay. Tony always said he'd never have got his football scholarship to Colorado State if it hadn't been for Clay taking them to the state finals their last year in high school. Of course, Clay won a scholarship, too, and he received offers to turn pro, which Tony didn't.'

Dallas capped her lipstick slowly. 'I always thought Kyle was the football star.'

'He was good, but Clay broke all his records. Kyle was two years older, and Clay never did much on the field until Kyle graduated. Tony always said that was because Clay didn't want to show Kyle up. I don't know. Kyle was the older, but it seemed as if he felt inferior to Clay, as if he was trying to prove that he was better than Clay. Maybe it was because Clay always knew what he wanted to do. Kyle was constantly searching. It's sad, because I don't think he ever found what he was looking for.' Vicky gave her a sidelong glance. 'I'm sorry about Alanna. Clay said you were close.'

'Yes.' Dallas shut her bag with a snap. She didn't want to talk about Alanna.

Clay was talking to a tall, distinguished, white-haired gentleman when Dallas and Vicky came back to the ballroom. 'Senator Jamison,' Vicky whispered. 'He's been after Clay for ages to get involved in politics.' At Dallas's look of surprise, Vicky explained,

'Clay's a natural. He's smart, personable, and his family's been here forever. Clay knows everybody.'

Clay reached out and pulled Dallas to his side, introducing her to the politician. 'Dallas lived in Alexandria before we were married,' Clay said.

'Maybe she'd like to go back there,' the older man said.

Clay laughed. 'Don't you listen to him, Dallas. He can talk the hide off a cow.'

The senator laughed with Clay. 'It's an art, my boy.' He turned to Dallas. 'All joshing aside, ma'am, Clay's a straight-shooter, and we need men like him in government.'

Dallas frowned. 'I don't think that——'

'Dallas is right,' Clay interrupted smoothly. 'Now isn't the right time. We've taken in my brother's child and she needs us. Politics would take too much time away from Nicky.'

The senator leaned back, nodding his head. 'Sure, Clay. Just don't forget about it.' He smiled at Dallas. 'You ever get homesick for the capital, drag Clay back east. Martha and I always have room for guests.' Accepting Dallas's thanks, he went on, 'Can I borrow your husband a minute?' Turning to Clay, he said, 'Harris and Turner would like your opinion on this little rustling problem that's been going on in your area.'

'Not at a party,' Clay protested.

Instinctively Dallas knew that Clay was protesting on her behalf. 'Go ahead,' she said. 'I'll be fine.'

'Course she will,' the senator boomed. 'Martha. Come take care of Clay's wife for a few minutes.'

Before Dallas could protest, she was drawn into conversations that ranged from recipes to world politics. Many of the party-goers were ranchers, but others were as likely to be bankers, lawyers, and doctors. She quickly discovered that even those who lived on isolated ranches kept up with current events.

A rancher whose black boots showed beneath his formal trousers explained it to her. 'A bad harvest in Russia, a famine in Africa, what's happening with the Common Market—all those things have a direct impact on us. We can't afford not to know what's going on all over the world. It's a lot different from the days back when our grandfathers were ranching, right, Terry?'

The man addressed allowed a tight-lipped smile. 'Lots of things are different now.' His voice chilled. 'For one thing, my family no longer owns a ranch. Thanks to Pete Dalton.'

'Now, Terry. You know no one else would have paid that outrageous price your dad was asking.' The rancher quickly changed the subject. 'Have you met Clay's new wife? Dallas, this is Terry Brock, Clay's cousin.'

'How do you do?' Dallas said, even as she wondered at Clay's neglecting to introduce his cousin to her.

The rancher was hailed from across the room and walked away. Terry Brock gave Dallas a chagrined smile. 'I should apologise for what I said about your father-in-law. The truth is, Ben was right, but when a kid grows up on a ranch that he thinks is going to be his some day, it's rather hard to swallow when it's sold from under him.' His eyes slid away from her, then back.

'I'm sorry.' Dallas didn't know what else to say. Terry had Clay's colouring but there the resemblance ended. He was attractive, but he lacked Clay's air of assurance. She tried to make conversation. 'What do you do now?'

'Work in a bank.' He grimaced. 'It's a living.'

'The hours are certainly better,' Dallas said brightly.

Terry's face stilled. 'That smile. It's Alanna's smile. I'd heard Clay married her cousin, but I didn't really believe it until now. Alanna was a special person.' He shoved his hands in his trouser pockets. 'She talked about you a lot. Did she ever mention me?'

Dallas shook her head. 'She talked very little about her life in Colorado.'

'Alanna wasn't meant to be hidden away on some ranch.' He glanced at Dallas and as quickly looked away. 'She confided in me... It was hard for her...the Daltons are the next thing to gods around here. How are you managing?'

'Wonderfully.'

'I'm glad to hear that. When I heard about the marriage, I worried about you. Knowing how Clay felt about Alanna...' Terry balanced back on his heels and studied the ceiling. 'Your marriage just seemed kind of sudden.' His gaze snapped back to her face, his eyes bright blue with inquisitiveness.

Suddenly Dallas felt like a specimen pinned beneath a magnifying glass for study. This man knew about Clay and Alanna and he was gleefully probing the depths of Dallas's knowledge. He was contemptible, disguising his maliciousness beneath a veneer of concern. Praying her face betrayed neither her shock nor her dislike, she said, 'Clay and I have known each other for years but, unfortunately, it took the tragedy to make us realise how much we meant to each other.'

'Love at second sight, right, sweetheart?' Clay pulled her back against him. 'How are you, Terry?'

'Fine. I've been chatting with your wife.' A pause seemed to give significance to his next words. 'About her cousin.'

Dallas felt Clay stiffen behind her, and she whirled in his arms. 'Darling.' Fiddling with his lapels, she shoved her lower lip out in an exaggerated pout and said, 'You aren't planning to waste that lovely music, are you?' She turned to Terry. 'You'll excuse us, won't you? Clay is so popular I have trouble getting him all to myself.'

Clay guided her on to the dance-floor. 'What did Terry say to you?' His voice was tense.

'Nothing, really. Mostly insinuations about Alanna.' She shuddered. 'He gave me the creeps.'

Clay pulled her tighter against his chest. 'I thought your eagerness was because you were dying to dance with me again.'

'Conceited, aren't you?' Dallas curved her arm around his neck. 'I was trying to get you away from your cousin. I swear, sparks flew between you two.'

'Terry hates all Daltons. His father made unwise investments and lost the family ranch. Terry blames my father for that. Unfairly, I might add.'

She caught his quick look at her. 'You didn't have to. I might disagree with Peter about cow heads, but I'd never believe he'd cheat someone. He has such an honest face.' The anniversary couple danced by, and Dallas felt a twinge of sorrow. 'He must be very lonely without your mother.'

'Nicky helps. That's one reason I couldn't let you take her so far away.' They danced in silence for a few minutes. 'Tonight hasn't been so bad, has it?'

'No.' Dallas smiled shyly up at him. 'Everyone has been very friendly. After the last party, I wasn't expecting that.'

Clay hesitated before saying, 'I'm afraid Alanna didn't fit in here. When everyone found out, through Vicky, what kind of person you really are, they liked you.'

'I guess I owe Vicky, then.'

The music stopped, and Clay smiled down at her. 'Vicky might have speeded things up, but the truth is you're a nice person who cares about other people. People respond to that.'

'What a nice thing to say.' His words sent a warm surge of pleasure over her. The music resumed, and she flowed back into his arms—strong arms that held her protectively against his hard body. Closing her eyes, she followed his lead with ease, as if they'd been dancing together for years. The lovely, haunting strains of music blotted out the conversation of those around them, insulating Clay and Dallas in their own private cocoon. His masculine aftershave enticed her closer and scented her every breath. Clay tucked her right hand against his chest, and his heart beat solidly beneath her palm. The heat from his body warmed her, surrounded her, and flooded her body with pleasurable sensation. When the music ended she forced up reluctant lids. Clay's face was close, his eyes deep blue, his lips drawing hers with magnetic intensity. Her eyelids dropped.

Clay cleared his throat. 'I'm glad you came.'

Dallas concentrated on one of his shirt studs. 'I-I'm glad you made me come. You were right.'

Clay laughed softly. 'Can I have that in writing?'

'No. You'd only use it against me.'

Vignettes from the evening kept replaying themselves in her mind, keeping her from sleep. Clay, so different in formal clothes. The senator, speaking of

Clay's integrity. And Vicky, revealing more of Clay's background. Dallas smiled in the darkened hotel room. Vicky might claim she thought Clay her ideal, but Dallas noticed that it was Tony, her own husband, whom Vicky constantly quoted. They were nice people.

She thought of the many others she'd met. They were all nice people. Nice people who obviously liked and respected Clay. A man couldn't buy that kind of respect. So what did that say about Clay? These people must know of Clay's relationship with Alanna. Did they excuse Clay and put the blame on Alanna, or did they ignore it because of Kyle's affair with Mercedes? Or maybe, like Clay, they simply felt what had happened in the past was best forgotten.

Dallas propped her head up on pillows. Was the rest of her life going to be dictated by something that had taken place before she married Clay. Clay had probably been having a torrid affair with Mercedes Irving. Why didn't that upset her? She rolled over on her stomach. Darn it, it did. She didn't want to think about Clay in bed with any other woman. Besides, it wasn't just the idea of Clay sleeping with Alanna— well, that, too—but that Clay could be so lacking in integrity. At least he had the decency to suffer for it. She didn't doubt that. His guilt and remorse punished him far more than she could. And since when was it up to her to throw stones? She was hardly perfect.

Dallas sat up and pulled her knees up to her chin. All marriages needed work, theirs more than most. Telling Clay she'd stay married to him, but refusing to throw her whole heart and soul into making their marriage work, wasn't fair to Clay or Nicky. Or even herself.

There was still a light showing beneath the connecting door. Reserving two rooms was Clay's way of granting her breathing-space. Earlier she'd been grateful to be spared the intimacy of dressing in the same room as Clay. Now she wished ... Propinquity would have taken the decision from her. They could talk over the party while Clay undid his tie. She could take her time removing the studs from the front of his shirt. Her breath caught at the thought of pushing the edges of his shirt aside, his skin warm and satin-smooth ...

All she'd packed was her flannel nightgown. Not exactly seductive. It dropped to the floor as she belted her chenille robe over her naked body.

She paused indecisively outside the connecting door. Maybe this wasn't the best way, considering what had happened the last time she'd gone to Clay with making ... with this on her mind. Tomorrow. They could have a rational discussion about the direction of their marriage. That way she wouldn't be taking Clay by surprise. She turned to flee back to her own bed.

'Change your mind?'

Dallas spun around. Clay was standing in the doorway, holding a magazine, his shirt hanging open over his trousers. Dallas swallowed hard. 'How ...?'

'Heard you. Did you want something?'

'No. That is ... it can wait.' His aftershave bridged the distance between them, speeding up her breathing.

Clay leaned against the door-jamb. 'Not so easy, is it?'

'What isn't?' Dallas clutched her robe tightly about her.

'Coming to someone's room.. Wondering what the other person wants, trying to decipher if the other person was sending out yes signals or definitely not. Worrying about what the other person will think if you do go, or what that person will think if you don't go. Wondering if you'll be rejected, and finally, thinking it would be better to put it off to another time.'

'I find it hard to believe that you——'

'Reminds me of the time when I was fourteen and trying to get up my courage to ask this blonde bombshell, Amy Lander, to a school dance. I was really hot for her.'

'Did she live up to your expectations?' Dallas asked, trying to ignore a tiny, jealous twinge.

'Never got my nerve up to ask her. I regret my lack of courage to this day.'

'You just made up that entire story.'

Clay straightened up, tossing his magazine to the floor, and strolled over to her. He adjusted the collar of her robe and then tugged her closer to his body. 'But the moral's true. Faint heart never won fair lad.'

'I think that's supposed to be fair lady.' Her pulse-rate accelerated at the look in Clay's eyes.

Clay's thumbs lightly traced her jawline. 'Same idea.'

'You're hardly a fair lad,' she breathed.

Clay stiffened. 'I assumed you were here because you'd decided to let the past alone. It's no good if you're going to constantly throw it in my face.' He dropped his hands.

'Clay!' Dallas grabbed at him as he turned, succeeding only in capturing his shirt. 'I didn't. I wasn't.' When he ignored her and tried to release his shirt, she tightened her grip. Clay yanked hard, but Dallas held firm. A loud rip echoed through the room. Consternation warred with a horrible urge to laugh.

'Damn it, Dallas. Do you know what I paid for that shirt?'

'Who cares about your stupid shirt?' She shoved him into his room to stand in front of his mirror. 'What do you see?'

'A man with a torn shirt and a wild woman behind him.'

'You see a man with dark hair. Dark hair, not fair.'

'Oh.' Clay's smile in the mirror was lop-sided. 'Expunging the past seems to be as difficult for me as for you.'

'What are we going to do about it?'

'We could try harder.' Clay turned her to face him, hands on her shoulders, his gaze locked with hers. 'I'm beginning to realise just how much I'd like us to succeed at this marriage business.'

'Yes,' Dallas whispered, mesmerised by blue eyes that deepened with some mysterious emotion.

'I hope you were planning to stay with me tonight.' Taking her silence for assent, he covered her mouth with his.

Dallas gripped the edges of Clay's shirt and swayed towards him, her lips parting in response to the gentle probing of his tongue. His intoxicating kisses tasted of champagne. Her breathing quickened, filling her nostrils with his scent. His hands slid from her shoulders, down her spine and back up her arms, and then tightened on her shoulders as he abandoned her mouth to trail warm kisses along her jawline and down her neck until his lips were pressed against the pulse which beat frantically at the base of her throat.

He lifted his head and threaded his fingers through her hair. 'All evening long I wanted to throw away those damned pins so I could do this while we were dancing.'

Dallas turned her head to rub her cheek against his hand. 'And I wanted to do this.' She slipped his shirt from his shoulders, her hands sliding up his chest. 'Now we need music.'

'Your wish is my command.' Clay moved away and then soft music flowed from the radio. 'My dance, I believe, Mrs Dalton.'

At first Dallas was content with Clay's arms wrapped tightly around her, his breath stirring the hair on her neck. Then, as his hands began gliding possessively over her body, her breasts grew heavy, the sensitive tips straining against her chenille robe. Dallas pressed against Clay, driven by the needs he was arousing. The knotted belt of her robe dug into her stomach, but that discomfort was minor compared to the ache deep within her.

'Your dress tonight drove me wild,' Clay said in a low voice. 'Every time you moved, it moulded another part of your body that I wanted to touch. And that zipper down the back.' He pressed her head back so he could see her face. 'Do you have any idea how tempting that was? All I could think about was you dancing naked in my arms.'

Dallas stepped from his arms and untied her belt, kicking it to one side as it fell. Her eyes holding Clay's, she shrugged the robe from her shoulders. Clay's eyes deepened to midnight-blue as the fabric slid to the floor with agonising slowness. She raised her arms. 'My dance, I believe, Mr Dalton.'

Clay scooped her up and carried her to his bed where he laid her gently down. 'Let's never stop dancing, Mrs Dalton.'

Dawn was still some hours away when Dallas awakened. Unfamiliar furniture shapes formed inky shadows in the dim room as her eyes grew accustomed to the dark. A heavy weight lay across her stomach, and someone was breathing warmly in her ear. Clay. Her pulse speeded up at the memory of their lovemaking.

Clay murmured in his sleep and then opened his eyes. Giving Dallas a blank look, he muttered, 'I should be going.'

Dallas brushed her hand over his face, closing his eyelids. 'No. Not you.' Clay rolled over, removing his arm from her. Sadness settled over Dallas. Clay's sleepy remark had reminded her of his reluctance to spend the entire night with her. Perhaps in time the passion they shared in the dark would survive the unrelenting light of dawn. Meanwhile, she would not jeopardise the fragile accord they'd reached last night. It would be unbearable if Clay's eyes held disappointment in the morning because she wasn't Alanna.

Judging from Clay's rotten mood the next day, he didn't need to see Dallas's face on his pillow to remind him of his lost love. At the breakfast table, he'd buried himself behind his newspaper. During the plane ride back to the ranch, he'd limited his conversation to terse directives. Once back at the ranch, he'd snarled at everyone who dared cross his path. By the end of the day he'd been offensive to every person on the ranch. It fell to Dallas's lot to follow him around, attempting to appease everyone. She should have known Clay would find out, and that the discovery would feed his wrath.

'Where do you get off telling Loren he could go to Denver?' he yelled, stomping into the dining-room. 'I run this ranch.'

Counting to ten, Dallas passed him his plate. 'You know very well that you told him last week he could have time off for his sister's wedding.'

'And who's going to do his work? Who's going to feed the cows tomorrow? Who's going to check up during the night on that damned cow that's having problems out in the barn? Jim was up all last night, even if he did make a hash of things.'

'He did not and you know it.' She passed him the rolls.

'Now you're a cattle expert, too, I suppose.'

'No. But when I was entering some information last week for you on the computer I saw where you'd noted that that cow had problems calving last year. As for Loren's other chores, I'm not working tomorrow so I can help out.'

'And we all know what a great help you are,' he mocked before switching his irritation to Nicky. 'What's the matter with your meat?'

'It's all fat,' Nicky said.

'It's perfectly good meat,' Clay said. 'Eat it.'

'Don't take your ill temper out on her,' Dallas said. 'If she doesn't like fat, she doesn't have to eat it.'

Clay shifted his frown towards her. 'Once you complained you couldn't breathe here without getting permission from the boss. It looks to me as if the boss doesn't have a damned thing to say about anything any more.' Clay leaned back in his chair and gave her a cold look. 'Just because you're a fun roll in the hay, I wouldn't let last night go to my head, Mrs Dalton.'

'I knew you'd finally get around to me. I'm who you're really mad at, aren't I? Why? Because of last night?' she asked, her voice coated with saccharin. 'Am I too much woman for you or merely the wrong woman?'

CHAPTER EIGHT

'YOU'RE the woman I'm stuck with,' Clay snarled. 'And don't you forget it!'

'That's it!' Dallas slammed her fork down on the table. 'I've lost my patience with you. You're acting like a spoiled brat who isn't getting his way for the first time in his life. And blaming me for it. You just might remember a couple of things,' she said, her chest heaving with rage. 'Number one, this marriage was your idea, not mine, and number two, you're not the only one who'd rather be married to someone else.'

Clay threw down his napkin. 'I'll be in my office.'

'And good riddance!' Dallas shouted childishly. She slumped back in her chair, her appetite gone. Clay's remarks had confirmed what she'd suspected all day. There was a delicious sense of irony in the situation—if only she could appreciate it. Clay had finally convinced her that she could overlook the past only to discover that he could not. There was no way this marriage could work.

'Clay's mad, isn't he?'

Nicky's small voice belatedly reminded Dallas of the child's presence. At the sight of Nicky's woebegone face, guilt flooded over Dallas. How many times the child must have seen and heard her parents enact this same type of scene. Dallas gave her a reassuring smile. 'Yes, Clay is mad. Sometimes grownups hurt inside so they say and do things they don't mean.' Walking around the table, she leaned down

and hugged Nicky. 'The important thing is that Clay
loves you.'

Her words to Nicky echoed in her head hours later.
Clay loved Nicky. That was the important thing.
Through the years there were bound to be many oc-
casions when the marriage chafed one or both of
them. Only last night they had promised to try harder
to help each other over the rough spots.

Clay was slumped in a well-worn leather chair, his
long legs stretched out in front of him, his eyes closed,
his entire body a picture of dejection.

'You didn't eat much dinner.' Her voice seemed un-
naturally high-pitched and loud in the book-lined
office. She set a tray on his desk. 'I brought you some
sandwiches and soup.'

'Why? Spreading oil on troubled waters?'

'I suppose. You must admit our marriage is pretty
troubled waters,' she added awkwardly, her back to
him as she perused his bookshelves. Clay's reading
material ranged from art to zoology, encompassing
everything from histories to biographies to philos-
ophies. Well-thumbed out-of-date novels shared shelf
space with the latest best-sellers. His tastes were
eclectic, and Dallas pounced happily on one of her
old favourites. 'May I borrow this?'

'Of course. You needn't ask.' After a long pause,
he came around his desk to where she was standing
and asked, 'You did enjoy the trip to Colorado
Springs, didn't you?'

The tone of his voice seemed to indicate more than
polite interest. Was he asking about the trip or was
he really asking about their sharing a bed? Dallas
turned to face him. 'You know I did.'

Clay studied her face for a long moment and then,
with a jerky movement unlike his usual easy motions,

reached up and awkwardly stroked her hair. 'There's no reason for you to feel as if the ranch is a prison. School spring break is coming up. I thought maybe we could take Nicky to DC for a few days. Take her to all the museums, show her the dinosaurs. I expect those fish houses you showed me in Alexandria would make her laugh.'

'Flounder houses,' Dallas said. 'I'm surprised you remember.'

Clay's hand stilled. 'I remember everything you showed me. You made history come alive for me. You could do the same for Nicky.' He hesitated. 'Of course, I'd be tagging along.'

'I thought . . .' Her eyes fell before his intense gaze. Now wasn't the time to bring up what Alanna had said. 'I'd like that.'

Clay cleared his throat. 'And this summer, I thought, if you wanted, you and Nicky could fly over and spend time with your folks in Europe. She's always considered them her grandparents.'

'Oh, Clay, could we? Mom and Dad would love that. You know they adore Nicky.' She frowned up into his face. 'What about you? Won't you be lonely without Nicky?'

Clay's attention was on the hair he was curling around his finger. When he spoke, his voice was almost diffident. 'I thought, after a while, I'd join you, and if Nicky is doing OK, maybe you and I might slip away for a few days together. I cheated you of the kind of wedding you deserved, but there's no reason why you have to be cheated out of a honeymoon. We should be able to find some kind of romantic spot over there.'

Happiness bubbled up within Dallas and she gave a light-hearted giggle. 'We should.' Catching Clay's hand with hers, she turned her head and pressed a kiss into his palm. 'What brought on this rash of ideas?'

'The same thing that sent you in here with a tray. This marriage of ours, it may be pretty tough going at times, but if we work at it ...' His palm slid from her lips to rest against her cheek. 'I want you to be happy. I owe——'

Dallas hushed him with a finger against his lips. 'You owe me nothing. Unless,' her fingers rubbed lightly over the contours of his mouth, 'it's an apology for hollering at me.'

Clay nipped at the tip of her finger with his teeth. 'What kind of apology did you have in mind, Mrs Dalton?' Sucking her finger into his mouth, he bathed the tingling tip.

Rescuing her finger from his diabolical tortures, Dallas unbuttoned his shirt and edged her hands inside where she rubbed her palms up and down his chest. Hard sinews lay beneath the warm skin. 'A contrite kiss might do.'

Clay nuzzled the pulse beneath her ear-lobe. 'I think that might be arranged,' he murmured and then his lips were on hers. Dallas spread her fingers wide on his bared chest. His heart pounded erratically beneath her hands. Could he be as affected as she? His warmth drew her lips from his and she pressed her mouth against the V of deep bronze at his throat. The rest of his skin was the colour of dark honey. Clay was still as she trailed her hands over his chest, sliding her fingers through the crisp hairs. The heat of his body burned her palms while his nipples hardened at her touch. Intrigued, she rolled the nubs between her thumbs and forefingers.

Clay's breathing quickened. 'Witch.'

She peered up at him from under lowered lids, provocative words on her tongue. They died unsaid at the flames in Clay's eyes. Slowly he unfastened and brushed aside her blouse so that only the merest wisp of lace separated them. He gave a low sound of pleasure, and then her swelling breasts were free. His fingers and then his mouth worked their magic until fiery bursts of desire surged from the sensitive tips and spread throughout her body. Her legs betrayed her with their weakness and she clung to Clay. His mouth returned to hers, his kisses deep and possessive. He lifted his head. 'Contrite enough for you?' His hands inside her clothing held her tightly against his bare chest.

Dallas shook her head against his chest. 'No.'

His chuckle was a deep rumble against her ear. 'Then you'll have to wait for later. I have to make one last check out in the barn. Then I'll do my best to appease you. I'll be damned if you aren't the bossiest, most demanding woman I've met.'

The smile in his voice took any sting from his words and Dallas snuggled contentedly against him. 'I'll wait,' she said.

Clay continued to hold her and gradually his breathing grew less erratic, his heartbeat slowed. 'I guess I have been a little grumpy,' he admitted.

'If you were a little grumpy, then the Rockies are a little mountain range. You've been an absolute stinker all day.'

'Yeah...' He hesitated. 'I didn't expect things to be so difficult.' His hands rubbed her back. 'I never thought much about it, but I supposed that some day, when the time was right, I'd meet a woman, fall in love, get married, have kids...' His hands stilled. 'I woke up this morning and felt as if I'd been cheated.

Silly, isn't it? I've got a good life. Doing what I want to do, friends, family, my health, Nicky... and I'm acting as if it's the end of the world because love didn't work out for me.' He looked down at her. 'I do want to apologise, because I messed it up for you, but I'll do my damnedest to make it up to you.'

'It's odd,' Dallas said to Molly days later as she rode the large horse across a brush-covered pasture. 'But I think I like Clay better since he's admitted suffering because he can never marry the woman he loved.' Clay had always seemed so in control of his life, it was somehow reassuring to discover that he, too, had his moments of fear and despair. When he'd stripped away his outer layer of invincibility, he'd allowed her to see the human being who struggled to deal with life on its own terms. Clay's vulnerability softened her anger, but it was his honesty that swept it away. Dallas had feared that he might regret revealing so much of himself to her, but if he did, he concealed the fact well.

Clay might deplore his loveless marriage, but there was no denying his sincere dedication towards making it work. He made no more objections to her hours at the school and even asked questions about her work. His own interests were far-ranging, and his dry sense of humour delighted Dallas. When she was honest with herself, she admitted that he'd always been good with Nicky. Maybe he didn't do things the way she would, but his love for Nicky more than compensated. Nicky adored him.

Molly stopped to nibble some dried grass, and Dallas nudged her impatiently. A chinook had passed through, bringing spring-like weather in the midst of winter, and Dallas was taking advantage of the warmth

and sunshine on a day she wasn't due at school. Her
thoughts returned to Clay. His employees as well as
his friends admired and respected him. In fact, Clay
was a paragon of virtues—with one exception...no,
she wouldn't think about that. Or the fact that
although Clay frequently joined her in her bedroom,
he always left once she'd fallen asleep. Dallas firmly
stamped out any faint prickles of discontent. Like
Clay, she had to accept the reality of their marriage.

Her mind elsewhere, Dallas paid no attention to
the small flock of mountain bluebirds perched on the
abandoned fence. The reins rested loosely in her hands
and her feet dangled free of the stirrups, giving her
about as much control over Molly as a sack of flour
hanging over the saddle. The birds took to the air in
an explosion of blue at Molly's approach. One flew
right at Molly, surprising the normally placid mare
into shying violently. Dallas was tossed from the
saddle to land with a painful jolt on the hard-packed
earth. The fall knocked the air from her and she
doubled up in agony.

Gradually the pain eased, and although her chest
still smarted, Dallas didn't think any ribs were frac-
tured. Her left side had taken the brunt of the fall
and, no doubt, bruises were already forming on her
hip and shoulder. Her wrist burned where she'd
scraped the ground as she landed, but her worst injury
appeared to be her left ankle, which throbbed agon-
isingly. She was again wearing borrowed boots, which
were too large, and her foot must have slipped inside
as she'd landed.

Dallas looked around. Molly was a few yards off,
her muscles trembling. Dallas called to her in a
soothing voice. The large horse walked hesitantly
forward until she loomed over Dallas. Talking quietly,

Dallas struggled to her knees. Gritting her teeth against the pain, she grabbed the mare's left stirrup. Molly side-stepped to the right, and Dallas lost her grip.

Striving for patience so she wouldn't frighten Molly, Dallas tried again. This time Molly rolled her eyes wildly, but she stood still as Dallas caught hold of the stirrup. Continuing to croon softly to the mare, Dallas pulled herself up until she was awkwardly balanced on her right foot. One hand on the saddle-horn and one hand clenching the back of the saddle, Dallas rested her forehead against the tooled leather.

Her body was damp with sweat inside her winter jacket and the ordeal had intensified the pain shooting through her ankle, but she still had to get in the saddle. Unable to put weight on her left foot, she found mounting impossible. Dallas tried pulling herself up, but her arms weren't strong enough and trying to leap up on one leg succeeded only in startling Molly and compounding the pain in her injured ankle.

Her situation was grim. Clay had gone to Pueblo and wasn't expected home until late. Nicky had gone to a friend's house for a birthday party after school. Jim had gone into town, and Dallas had told Sara that she might ride over to Peter's. Her father-in-law, however, wasn't expecting her. It might be hours before it occurred to anyone that Dallas was missing. And once the sun dipped behind the mountains it was going to be very cold.

She looked around. The Spanish Peaks had been behind her while she rode. If she headed back towards them . . . Taking a deep breath, Dallas gave the mare a gentle swat. 'It's up to you.' Molly obediently started off, dragging Dallas with her. Yards, miles, hours, days—Dallas quickly lost track of distance and time.

The strain on her arms was excruciating and her ankle ached intolerably, but she doggedly hung on to the saddle.

Closing her eyes, she saw Clay standing in her living-room in Alexandria. 'It's too much to ask of a woman,' he said. She would show him. 'I'll take care of you,' he promised. Then he smiled. 'Tenderfoot. Falling off Molly.' His eyes were soft and teasing as he faded away.

'Don't go,' Dallas begged.

His place was taken by a giggling Nicky. 'I like Clay. He's so silly sometimes.'

'Clay is dependable,' Mercedes said.

'A date with Clay is winning the lottery,' Vicky added.

The three began to grow dim. 'No,' Dallas cried.

Alanna was there, concern on her face. 'Hang on, Dallas. Think about Nicky. You promised.'

'What about Clay?'

'I can't give you Clay,' Alanna said, her image beginning to dissolve. 'You must fight for him.'

'Wait,' Dallas sobbed.

'Faint heart never won fair lad.' Clay was back. 'Don't you want to win me, Dallas?' Taking her assent for granted, he bent to kiss her lips.

His mouth was hard and cold. Dallas opened her eyes. She was lying on the ground, her arm over her face. She looked around in confusion. Molly was gone. Lengthening shadows moved across the pasture while the setting sun painted the sky with splashes of rose. The Spanish Peaks seemed no closer. Dallas shivered inside her down jacket. The ranch could be anywhere south of her. One pasture was much like another to her. She'd paid little attention to their meandering route, relying on Molly's homing instinct. It was even possible that the ranch was just over that knoll.

If it was, she'd feel pretty silly when Clay found her. On her hands and knees, Dallas dragged herself laboriously up the incline, becoming more and more convinced that she'd see the ranch outbuildings below. At the top of the knoll, Dallas almost cried with disappointment. No welcoming ranch lights penetrated the dusk. Only scrub oat and grama grass rose from the pasture. Her breath caught in her throat as one and then another of the scrub oat took on bovine dimensions. Heading slowly, inexorably in her direction were cows. Lots of cows. Dallas looked over her shoulder. Absorbed in her climb up the hill, she'd failed to notice the stock pond. The stock pond for which the cows were headed, with her injured body the only obstacle in their path.

Thirty minutes later found the cows milling around the pond and Dallas wedged uncomfortably up against a solitary piñon pine while she picked gravel and burrs from her knees. Finally, convinced of the cows' lack of interest in her, Dallas gave in to exhaustion and curled up in a ball on the ground.

Cold, her ankle throbbing painfully, Dallas exhorted Clay to hurry. As time passed, she began to mentally bargain with him. If he came in the next ten minutes, she'd never yell at him again. Then she promised to never again mention the past. She fell asleep vowing that she'd become the perfect wife, making up to Clay for all his unhappiness.

She didn't know what woke her. The air was cold, her body stiff and cramped. When she stretched, pain shot from her ankle and nausea rose in her throat. Night had fallen, but a full moon bathed the landscape with light. Dallas heard the tortured sound of a truck in low gear attacking the rough pasture, and her body went limp with relief. Clay. Her mouth was parched and the noise from the truck's engine swallowed her cry.

The headlights were out on the truck. Clay must be afraid of startling the cows. She wasn't keen on the idea herself. A stampeding herd headed towards her...Dallas shuddered. The truck stopped at the end of a nearby draw she remembered seeing earlier. Dallas crawled in that direction, no longer tempted to yell to Clay. The cattle were already restless, their hoofs stamping the hard ground as they headed away from her down into the draw. The dark shadow of a man separated from the blackness cast by a patch of scrub oat directly in her path. 'Clay!'

The man whirled at her voice. 'Who's there?'

'It's me, Dallas.'

Clay didn't move. 'What are you doing here?'

'I fell off Molly,' Dallas said, confused by Clay's attitude. 'Weren't you looking for me?'

There was a pause. 'Are you hurt?'

'My ankle. I think I sprained it.' The man's face was in shadow. 'You're not Clay,' she suddenly guessed.

'Are you expecting him?'

The voice sounded familiar. Dallas strained to see the man's face. 'Yes.'

The man chuckled. 'No, you're not. He went to Pueblo.'

'How do you know?'

'He ate breakfast at the café before he left. News travels fast in a small town.'

'He's back by now,' Dallas said.

'How would he know where you are even if he was back?'

'My horse went home. Clay will be looking for me.'

'But will he know where to find you?'

'Of course, I——'

'You're lying. Can you walk? No, not with a sprained ankle,' he answered his own question. 'I'll be back.'

The man disappeared down into the draw and over the sound of the moving cattle Dallas thought she heard snatches of conversation. There were at least two men.

A pick-up pulled up beside her, and a man got out. Dallas gasped. No wonder she hadn't been able to recognise him. He was wearing a ski mask that covered all but his mouth and eyes. 'What—what . . . who are you . . . where are you taking me?'

He picked her up and set her on the front seat of the pick-up. 'Somewhere you can wrap up in a blanket.'

Minutes later they parked in front of the old cabin. Dallas had used those minutes to think furiously. 'You're stealing Clay's cows, aren't you?'

'It's safer to mind your own business.' The man unbolted the cabin door and carried Dallas inside, depositing her on the covered bunk.

'How did you know about this place?'

'You ask too many questions,' he said. 'You'll be OK here, if a little uncomfortable.'

She couldn't let him leave. Not when he was stealing Clay's cows. 'I'm freezing. Can't you start a fire in the fireplace?'

'And have someone out here immediately to investigate? If you're cold, use the blanket. I'll call Clay in the morning and tell him where you are.' He started for the door.

The angry sneer in his voice as he'd said Clay's name sparked Dallas's memory and suddenly she knew where she'd heard the voice before. 'Terry Brock.' The name popped out before she could consider the consequences.

He turned and looked down at her. 'I'm real sorry you said that, Dallas.' He tugged the knit cap from his head.

She scrunched into the far corner of the bunk. 'Why are you stealing Clay's cows? He's a relative of yours.'

'That didn't stop Pete from stealing our ranch.'

'You admitted yourself that he paid more than it was worth.'

'You can't use logic with Terry.'

'Clay!' Intent on Terry, she hadn't seen the cabin door open. 'I'm so glad to see you.'

Standing in the doorway, holding a lantern, Clay didn't take his eyes from his cousin. 'You OK, Dallas?'

'I'm fine. That is, a little sprain... How did you...?'

'Sara saw Molly return to the barn. When you weren't with my dad, Sara tracked me down in Pueblo.'

'Terry found me and brought me here,' she said.

'A stroke of luck you happened on her,' Clay said, his voice hardening at the word 'happened'. 'Just out for an evening ride in the moonlight?'

'That's right.'

'No, Clay, he was——'

'Never mind, Dallas. I know what he was doing.' Clay kicked the door shut and walked into the cabin. He set the lantern on the table, banishing the shadows to the corners.

'You can't prove anything,' Terry sneered.

'I was looking for Dallas when I ran across your little operation. It was interesting, but not as interesting as you carrying a woman to your pick-up. Why bring her here?'

Dallas could sense the rage beneath Clay's words. She couldn't blame him. Terry had been stealing his cows.

'Not why you think,' Terry said. 'I wouldn't hurt her. Not Alanna's cousin.'

'If that's true, you won't mention Alanna,' Clay said. An unspoken message seemed to pass between the two men.

'Now what?' Terry asked.

'I'll make a bargain with you. I'll forget about tonight, and you'll cease your rustling activities. I'm not the only one suspicious of you, you know.'

'Clay, you can't——'

'Be quiet, Dallas. This is between me and Terry.'

Terry smiled insolently. 'The truck's probably already loaded.'

'There are search parties out for Dallas. Think you can evade all of them?' Clay asked.

'I'll manage,' Terry said.

Clay shrugged. 'Your gamble. I'll do nothing this time, and you keep your mouth shut. About everything.'

Terry sketched an airy salute. 'Your wish and all that.'

'Don't cross me on this,' Clay warned.

Even in the shadowed cabin Dallas could see the bleak look in Terry's blue eyes. 'Don't worry. I can keep a secret.' He hesitated. 'Apparently so can you.'

What Terry and Clay weren't saying suddenly seemed significant to Dallas. This wasn't the first time that Terry had indicated that Alanna was special to him. And how did Terry know there would be a blanket in an abandoned cabin? And why did he refuse to tell Dallas how he knew about the cabin? She couldn't ask him why Alanna was so special to him. There was only one question that he might answer. 'What does D.P. stand for?'

Both men were puzzled by the question. Terry answered it. 'The Dusty Penny, my family's ranch. D.P. was the brand.' He gave Clay a wry look. 'Well, Cuz, see you around.'

The silence was loud following Terry's departure. Mingled hope and doubt took root with Terry's answer. Was it possible that Terry, not Clay, had been Alanna's lover? Clay wasn't Kyle's only flesh and blood. Terry was Kyle's cousin. Had she been too quick to condemn Clay?

Clay was at her side. He reached down. 'Which ankle?'

Dallas gasped with pain as he touched it. 'Why did you let Terry go?'

'What did you expect me to do? Beat him up?' Pulling off the boot, he gently examined her ankle.

Dallas bit her bottom lip. 'You could call the sheriff . . . get the licence number of the truck . . .' She hardly knew what she was saying.

Clay released her leg and wrapped the blanket around her. 'What happened?'

'Some birds startled Molly and I fell off.'

'Tenderfoot.' He hoisted her up and then his arms tightened painfully around her and he buried his face in the curve of her shoulder. 'You scared the hell out of me. Speeding back to the ranch, I kept seeing you, lying hurt somewhere, and when we didn't find you right away and it got dark . . .' He cleared his throat. 'I'd better get you to the doctor.'

Dallas couldn't think of anything to say as Clay carried her out to his pick-up. She knew he was remembering his mother. Finally she changed the subject back to Terry. 'You've got to stop him.'

'I can't.' Clay went around the truck and settled behind the wheel. 'He is my cousin.'

'That's not why you let him go. You don't want anything to blacken the sacred Dalton name.'

'Drop it.' Clay slammed his pick-up into gear.

Dallas stared blindly out into the night. Her foot ached abominably and her throat was raw with unshed tears. It wasn't the Dalton name that Clay was protecting. He might not have been the D.P. of Alanna's diary, but he had obviously cared a great deal for her. Why else would he be protecting her name? That was what Clay's deal with Terry was all about. Cows in exchange for Terry's silence about his affair with Alanna. 'He'll do it again,' she said. 'It's nothing more than blackmail. You may as well turn the whole ranch over to him now.'

Ignoring her, Clay spoke into his CB radio. 'Dad, can you hear me? I have Dallas. Call everyone in.'

'She OK?'

'Looks like a sprained ankle. I'm taking her into town.'

'How'd she go and do that?'

'Molly dumped her.'

'Any dude could handle Molly. How come you let her ride without a keeper? Dadburned woman. She's more trouble than——'

'She's also sitting right here,' Clay said wryly.

Peter snorted. 'Tell her she ought to spend less time messing with perfectly good houses and more time on a horse.'

Clay didn't look at Dallas. 'Dad always gets a little testy when he's worried. It doesn't mean anything.'

Dallas wrapped the blanket tighter around her. 'It doesn't matter.' She knew what Clay's father thought about her.

'Clay? You still there?' The panic in Peter's voice came clearly over the radio.

'Nicky's gone!' Sara must have grabbed the speaker from Peter. 'I went up to tell her that Dallas is OK, and she's not anywhere in the house. Her coat is gone, but...' Sara's voice caught on a sob. 'She's in her nightgown and slippers.'

Sara's announcement signalled the beginning of a nightmare. Dallas insisted on staying with Clay until Nicky was found. The CB crackled again and again with voices as one area and then another was unsuccessfully covered.

'Why would she leave? Where would she go?' Dallas asked.

They could almost hear Sara wringing her hands in distress. 'I tried to keep it from her about Dallas being missing, but she must have heard Pete talking to the sheriff.'

'But Nicky wouldn't go looking for me.' Dallas appealed to Clay for reassurance. 'Would she?'

'No.' He hesitated. 'I think she ran away.'

'But why?'

Clay's face was white and bleak in the moonlight. 'Lisa's mom brought Nicky home about the time I was organising the search party. Nicky isn't dumb. She knew something was going on. She kept bugging me, and I told her I had to go out. She wanted to come along, wouldn't take no for an answer. I snapped at her, said I was busy and sent her to her room. I should have seen how upset she was and been more patient with her.'

'You can't blame——'

'The hell I can't.' He shrugged her hand off his arm. 'You were right. I failed Kyle and now I've failed his daughter.'

'Berating yourself won't find Nicky.'

'What will? You're the one with all the bright ideas. Where would she go?'

Dallas ignored the anger in Clay's voice, knowing it was directed less at her than at his own frustration. 'We need to concentrate on how Nicky would think. Where she would run.'

Clay drummed his fingers on the steering-wheel. 'Dad's at our house. Nicky's friends live so far away that even Nicky would know she couldn't walk there.' He went back to the CB and checked to make sure no horses were missing.

'Teddy,' Dallas said suddenly. At Clay's perplexed frown, she explained. 'The baby calf. Nicky's crazy about him. Maybe she ran to the barn. When kids are upset they frequently head for their pets because pets are so accepting.'

'But the calf's not in the barn—Nicky knows that. I told her yesterday that we were taking him and his mother back out to the pasture. I even told her which pasture he...' Clay's gaze locked with Dallas's. 'Do you think it's possible?' At her nod he hit the brakes, bringing the truck to a screeching halt. They were soon headed back in the other direction.

Straining to find one small child in the enormous landscape, Dallas crossed her fingers and prayed, afraid to ask Clay if there were bears or wolves in the area. Suddenly she spotted the forlorn little figure stumbling over the rocky ground. 'There!'

Clay wrenched the pick-up around to head in the direction of her pointing finger. The truck had barely halted before he was running to sweep Nicky up in his arms, hugging her as if he'd never let her go. Dallas opened her door and Clay lifted Nicky over her, depositing the child in the middle of the seat. 'She's chilled, but OK,' he said, his voice hoarse with the strain.

Dallas struggled from her blanket and wrapped it around Nicky while Clay jumped in and turned the heater on full blast. Taking Nicky's feet on her lap and warming them between her hands, Dallas was giddy with relief. 'These aren't toes, they're piggicyles,' she teased. Nicky's nightgown was wet around the bottom. Dallas stripped it from the child and rebundled her in the blanket. Nicky snuggled up against Dallas as Clay notified everyone that the child had been found and that he was taking her and Dallas to the doctor to be checked. Dallas knew she ought to scold Nicky, but she was so thankful the little girl was safe that all she could do was sit and hug her.

'Are you mad at me, Dallas? Is that why you went away?' Nicky asked in a little voice.

'Silly girl. I didn't go away. I fell off Molly and hurt my foot so Clay had to come to get me. Wasn't that silly of me, to fall off Molly? Is that why you left the house? You know better than to wander around outdoors after dark.' She squeezed the child. 'Everyone was so worried about you.'

'Wanted to talk to Teddy. Everybody was too busy.'

Dallas caught the stricken look on Clay's face. 'You know Clay loves you, don't you, Nicky?' At Nicky's nod, Dallas said, 'Clay was scared that I might be hurt. When grown-ups are afraid, they holler and yell so other people won't know how scared they are.'

'Why?'

'I don't know. Grown-ups are kind of silly sometimes,' Dallas said.

Nicky giggled. 'You think all peoples are silly. You called me silly 'cuz I thinked you'd gone, you're silly 'cuz you fell off Molly, and now Clay is silly, too.'

'Clay is just happy to have his favourite little girl back,' Clay said. 'Honey, don't ever scare me like that again.' He reached over and tousled her hair. 'I'm sorry that I yelled at you. Friends again?'

'Friends,' Nicky solemnly agreed.

Friends, Dallas thought drowsily several hours later, as the pain medicine the doctor had prescribed took effect. Nicky, exhausted, had fallen asleep in Dallas's arms on the way back to the ranch. Clay had handed her over to his father while he'd helped Dallas from the truck. The doctor had given Dallas crutches, but Clay had insisted on carrying her to her bedroom. Then he'd tucked Nicky into bed while Sara had helped Dallas. Now everyone was gone. Except for the three of them. Three friends. Brother, cousin, niece. Father, mother, child. Husband, wife...

Dallas's eyelids felt leaden. Life hadn't been easy since she'd moved out here. She and Clay were totally different people whose only common ground was Nicky. On second thoughts, maybe their problem was that they were too much alike. Clay was used to running things and, as an only child, she was used to having things done her way. And yet, in spite of the many strikes against them, Dallas felt confident of their success—for the first time. She smiled to herself. They were too stubborn to admit to failure.

She fought off sleep. Clay said he'd be back after Nicky fell asleep. Perhaps he would lie on the bed and hold her in his arms and the sound of his heart would lull her to sleep. A little giggle escaped her. Lying in Clay's arms was not normally the prelude to sleep. At least not immediately. Her pulse quickened in recollection. Clay was a very satisfactory lover. More than satisfactory.

Her bedroom door opened. 'How's the ankle?' Clay asked.

'Hurts, but I'll live. How's Nicky?'

'Asleep,' Clay said absently, as he prowled restlessly around her room.

Dallas frowned at Clay's back. He was obviously still perturbed about Nicky's running away. 'I'll bet being a husband and father is more exciting than you anticipated,' she said lightly.

Clay jammed his hands in his pockets, his shoulders taut with tension. He spoke without turning. 'I want you to file for a divorce.'

CHAPTER NINE

'DIVORCE,' Dallas echoed in a hollow voice. 'Why?'

'Because this whole marriage idea is asinine.'

'Isn't it a little late to come to that conclusion?'

Clay whirled. 'Are you pregnant?'

'No! It's just...I can't think...' She rolled her head in anguish on her pillow.

Clay moved to stand by the bed. 'I'm sorry. You're in pain, and this is a bad time to bring the subject up.' He bent and pressed a warm kiss on her forehead. 'We'll discuss it when you're feeling better.'

Dallas could only stare blindly at the closed bedroom door. The pain medicine addled her brain, and she was so tired. Divorce. The horrible word whirled around and around inside her head. What a muddle she'd made of this marriage. She'd been so busy trying to maintain her identity and keep Clay from steam-rolling over her that she hadn't even considered his feelings. She'd redecorated his house, argued with him over raising Nicky and interfered with his ranch. A tear slid down her face. No wonder Clay had decided to get rid of her. What good was she to him? If he couldn't have Alanna, he at least deserved a wife who could stay on a horse.

The events of the day belatedly caught up with her, and tears flowed unchecked down her cheeks. Falling off Molly. Hurting her ankle. Lost. The beastly cows. Terry frightening her with his ski mask and threatening to leave her in the cabin. The terror when Nicky had disappeared. And now Clay serving notice that he didn't want her around any more. Not until Dallas had wept herself into exhaustion did she fall asleep.

Only to suffer horrible nightmares. Huge, horned beasts and faceless creatures with piercing eyes tormented her slumbers. One fiend had Terry's sneering voice and he laughed maliciously as she tried to escape from him. Clay was in the distance, but, no matter how hard she ran, she couldn't reach him. 'Clay!'

'It's OK, I'm here.'

Dallas blinked open her eyes. The room was dark and she could barely make out Clay's form leaning over the bed. 'Why are you still up?' she whispered. 'Is something wrong with Nicky?'

'No. I was sitting here,' he nodded towards the chair across the room, 'in case you needed anything.' He helped her sit up and handed her a glass and a pain pill. 'How's the ankle?'

She swallowed the water gratefully. 'Hurts.' Lying back down, she said, 'I'm sorry for all the trouble I caused. Sara said you organised an extensive search party.'

Clay pulled the blanket up over her shoulders. 'I'll never be able to face my neighbours again. Clay Dalton's wife falling off a horse.'

'I'm sorry, I——'

'I was teasing you, Dallas, trying to take your mind off your pain. Lord knows it was no joke when Molly came home alone.'

'No,' she said bitterly. 'That's not the joke. The joke is us. Thinking we could make this work.' She recalled her earlier thoughts. 'You expected too much of me.'

Clay walked back to the chair. His disembodied voice was harsh. 'I guess I did. If it makes you feel any better, you were right all along. A marriage is

more than two people living in the same house, sharing
the same bed. When there's no love between a husband
and a wife, then the marriage is a sham, unfair to
either partner.' He hesitated before adding, 'Unfortunately, love can't be forced.'

'No,' Dallas said listlessly. Clay was telling her that
he could never love her. She thought of the evening
he'd confessed that in his office. Only then he'd
thought it didn't matter. Tears trickled down her
cheeks, and then her eyes slowly closed as she drifted
back into a pill-induced sleep.

Her room was bright with sunshine when a giggle
sounded outside the bedroom door. Dallas opened her
eyes. Nicky grinned at her before yelling, 'She's
awake!'

'How are you this morning?' Dallas asked.

Nicky skipped into the room. 'Guess what? Today
is Saturday and I don't have school and Clay and I
are playing nurse.' She giggled again. 'You're our
patient.'

Dallas smiled. 'I'm not sure I like the sound of that.'

Clay shoved open her bedroom door with his foot
just in time to hear her comment. 'Do I detect a certain
lack of confidence in our abilities?' he asked, placing
an enormous tray in front of her as she sat up in bed.
Odd bits of china and crystal held coffee, juice, eggs,
toast, jam, butter and bacon.

Dallas looked at Clay in dismay. 'Sara shouldn't
have come on her day off. Cereal or something would
have been fine.'

'Did you hear that, Nicky? Dallas thinks Sara fixed
this magnificent breakfast,' Clay said.

'Me and Clay cooked,' Nicky said proudly. 'I made
the toast and poured the juice. Clay let me pick out
the dishes. Don't they look pretty?' She surveyed the

tray complacently and then perched on Clay's lap, both of them watching Dallas with expectant faces.

Dallas gave them a weak smile. She hoped she could choke down something. A minute later she was practically inhaling the food. 'This tastes wonderful. You shouldn't have gone to so much trouble,' she mumbled around a mouthful of eggs.

Clay grinned. 'You don't have to eat it if it's that bad.'

Dallas wiped her mouth with her napkin and pushed aside her empty dishes. 'I never did eat dinner last night,' she offered in apology for her table manners. 'Did you really fix this?'

'Come on, Dallas. The man who would starve to death without a woman around is nothing more than a tired cliché these days,' Clay said. 'I can even wash my own socks.'

'No wonder you don't need a wife,' Dallas said.

Her comment wiped the grin from Clay's face. 'I wasn't sure if you would remember our conversation from last night.'

'Some things are difficult to forget.' She twisted her wedding-ring. 'This little experiment has certainly given me plenty to remember. Blizzards, cattle rustlers, squatters' cabins, bucking broncos.'

Clay gave her a twisted smile. 'Did you hate it so much?'

'It was all right.' Not for a million dollars would she admit how much she had loved her stay and how much she would miss the ranch. Clay would only think that she was begging him to change his mind about the divorce. Her lips trembled. 'Once I said it was no place for a child. I was wrong about that.'

Clay glanced at the small girl still on his lap. 'We'll have to talk about Nicky.'

At the sound of her name, Nicky hopped down. 'Guess what, Dallas? This afternoon, if you're good enough to leave alone, me and Clay are going to the Bealls'. Clay said they have some new kittens and I get one. For my very own.'

Dallas couldn't help but respond to the child's enthusiasm. 'That's wonderful.' She smiled at Clay. 'It's a great idea.'

'You gave it to me. There are so many animals around here that it never occurred to me until last night that Nicky doesn't have one that's hers. Every kid should have a pet. Didn't you?'

Dallas shook her head. 'I always wanted a cat, but my folks thought it would be too difficult, moving as much as we did.'

Clay set her crutches beside the bed and picked up the tray. 'Nicky and I are going to do the dishes...yes,' he said over the child's wail, 'we are. You can come up and entertain Dallas afterwards.' He looked at Dallas. 'Holler if you need anything.'

Clay was good with Nicky. Dallas would miss the child, but she needn't worry about her. Maybe Clay wouldn't always do things the way Dallas would, but he loved Nicky and would take good care of her. Nicky would be all right. An aching void opened before Dallas, and her fingers curled with pain. Surely Clay would understand that Nicky had already lost too many people in her life to lose Dallas, too. He wouldn't make Dallas give Nicky up totally. He'd already forced Dallas to give up so much. No—that wasn't true. Clay hadn't forced her to marry him. Not really. She'd wanted to do it for Nicky. Her hands relaxed. Clay would be fair; he'd understand that it was in Nicky's best interests for her and Dallas to maintain contact. Maybe Dallas could even visit them on the ranch.

She picked up a book to read, but it was soon abandoned as she lost herself in daydreams. She was riding a big black stallion named Dynamite. Clay was on crutches and she was feeding the cows for him. Clay was thanking her for convincing Terry to stop rustling. Women at a party were saying that Clay had been crazy to divorce a wife such as Dallas. A wife who could ride with the best of them, who rescued cows in a blizzard, who whipped up gourmet food for a neighbourhood party, and who had all the men wishing they could sleep with her. And Clay. Bemoaning the fact that he'd sent her away. Begging her to come back. She smiled with sleepy satisfaction. Let him beg.

'Are you awake, Dallas?' Nicky was peeking around the door. When she saw Dallas's opened eyes, she bounced into the bedroom carrying a calico kitten. 'His name is Patches,' she said, holding him out.

Dallas dutifully admired the kitten before giving him back to Nicky as Clay came in.

'This little fellow,' Clay set a honey-coloured kitten on the covers beside Dallas, 'followed us home, miaowing all the way.'

'He was saying, "I want to live with Dallas, I want to live with Dallas".' Nicky giggled with excitement. 'He didn't really follow us home. Clay gotted him for you. Are you surprised?'

'I certainly am.' Dallas held up the warm, furry bundle. The kitten yawned in her face, his pink mouth opening wide. 'He's so sweet. Is he really for me? What's his name?'

'He's yours. You name him,' Clay said.

Dallas set the kitten down on the covers and watched him sneak up and pounce on her book. 'He's almost the same colour as Molly,' she said. 'What kind of horse did you say she is?'

'Buckskin, mostly.'

'That's it, then. I'll name him Buck.' She cuddled the tiny animal in her lap. 'What do you think, Buck? How's that for a real western name?' The kitten was fast asleep. Dallas gave Clay a quick look. 'Thank you.'

He shrugged off her thanks. 'The Bealls had four kittens left. I was lucky to get out of there with only two.' He watched Nicky scamper off to her room to play with her kitten. 'About Nicky,' he began abruptly.

Dallas had been petting the kitten, but now her hand froze, and anger burst from within her. 'I suppose this kitten is supposed to be compensation for my big sacrifice,' she said.

'I'm sorry. I know you gave up a lot...' Clay gestured helplessly, his shoulders sagging. 'You'll meet someone, fall in love and be able to provide Nicky with a home and a real family.'

'And until I marry this mythical man, Nicky stays with you?'

'No. I won't fight for custody. You're right. You're better at this parenting stuff.' He paused in the doorway, his back to her. 'I know you'll be fair about her visiting...and stuff. I...my dad...will miss her.' He disappeared from view.

Dallas slumped against the pillows, weak with astonishment. Clay was conceding custody, giving her what she wanted. Then why did she feel so miserable? The answer came quickly. She didn't want to leave, even with Nicky. She didn't want a divorce.

Clay had totally disrupted her life, practically forcing her to marry him. She'd changed her whole life for him and now he was rejecting her sacrifice. Damn him. He was arrogant, he was bossy, he was...strong. Not just physically. His was the kind of strength that was supported by quiet self-confidence. Tall in the saddle, Clay was the epitome of the rugged western hero, yet his masculinity was secure enough that he had no qualms about cooking her breakfast or confessing to fears or apologising.

The kitten had looked so tiny in Clay's large hands, yet so secure. Nicky instinctively trusted Clay, openly showering him with her love. Even Dallas had never doubted that Clay would come to her rescue when she'd fallen from Molly. She'd needed him and he'd come. As she would always need him. Clay was fun, interesting, intelligent, hard-working, honest, and the perfect husband for Dallas.

Tears trickled from her eyes. When had Clay Dalton become essential to her life? How could she have fallen in love with him without even knowing it? Love. Suddenly it was simply there. The way a smile crinkled his face. The tenderness in his eyes when he talked to Nicky. His concern over Dallas's happiness. His willingness to sacrifice his future for his brother's child. Dallas's eyes slowly closed. The fluid way he moved. The way his mouth felt against hers.

She couldn't swallow over the lump in her throat. Of all the stupid things to do—to fall in love with her husband. Her husband who wanted to divorce her because he couldn't love her. Because he had already given his heart to a dead woman. A pain almost too intense to bear washed over her.

The kitten roused Dallas from her self-pitying reverie as he miaowed plaintively at the closed bedroom door. Dallas glanced doubtfully at her plaster-encased ankle. Only a sprain, the doctor had said, but he had still put on a cast. She wasn't very steady on her crutches yet, but she ought to at least be able to make it to the head of the stairs. Buck disappeared before she reached the staircase, and Dallas paused to search for him. Below her, the door to Clay's study was open. Before Dallas could call to Clay, she heard his father speak.

'Clay, I don't mean to stick my nose into your business——'

'Then don't,' Clay interrupted his father.

For a few moments, the silence was broken only by the clinking of glasses.

'There's something strange about your finding Dallas in that old cabin,' Peter finally said. 'When I asked her about it, she got a funny look on her face and mumbled something about Molly taking her there. I find that downright odd that a horse would go to an empty cabin instead of heading for the barn.'

'Are you accusing Dallas of arranging to meet someone there?' Clay asked in a cold voice.

'Good golly, no. I wouldn't believe it if you told me she did. I like that gal. She's got gumption. Besides, she has an honest face if I ever saw one.'

Clay gave a short laugh. 'Believe it or not, that's what she said about you.'

'Did she?' Peter sounded pleased. 'Well, then, how did she get to the cabin?'

Clay's next words caught Dallas by surprise. 'Dad, did you ever wonder what Kyle did all those nights he spent away from the ranch?'

'Holed up in some motel and drank, I suppose. Anything to get away from that bitch he married.'

'He was sleeping with Mercedes Irving,' Clay said flatly.

Peter didn't answer for a long time. When he did, his voice was heavy with pain. 'Yeah. I wondered. Saw his car over there a couple of times when it shouldn't have been. How'd you know?'

'He let it slip once. The point is, somehow Alanna found out. And she decided tit for tat.'

There was another long silence before Peter asked, 'Who?'

'Terry Brock.'

'That lazy, no-account... Why him?'

'Can you think of anyone who would infuriate Kyle more?' Peter must have shaken his head. 'Neither could Alanna. I wasn't sure, but I suspected. They were meeting at the cabin. Molly remembered hay was cached there and she took Dallas there once. However, the other night,' Clay's voice hardened, 'Terry took her there.'

'Terry and Dallas?'

'No, dammit. Terry was helping himself to a few of my cattle when he ran across Dallas.' Clay made a disgusted sound. 'Apparently he helped her as a sort of memorial to Alanna.'

'Rustling cattle and you didn't sic the sheriff on him!'

'I told him I'd let him go this time, if he kept his mouth shut about him and Alanna.'

'Listen, Clay. Everyone knows Kyle was drinking that night because he was furious with his wife. He had probably found out about Terry. She was a harlot. Why would you protect her?'

'I'm not protecting Alanna. I'm protecting Dallas. Others might have suspected Terry and Alanna. I don't want anyone to get the wrong idea about Dallas. Besides...' Clay hesitated. 'Dallas idolised her cousin, and she thought Terry the worst kind of slime. How would she feel if she knew the two of them were having an affair?'

'Don't you think it's about time Dallas opened her eyes to the kind of woman Alanna was?'

'Why don't you tell her?' Clay's laugh was mocking. 'That's what I thought.' He paused. 'Dallas accused me of refusing to see what Kyle had become. She was right. Maybe Dallas is blind as a bat when it comes to Alanna, but Kyle was certainly no candidate for sainthood after that accident.'

'Yeah, but that woman——'

'No. We have to quit lying to ourselves. We saw enough of them to know they were happy before Kyle resigned from the Navy. Their problems stemmed from his plane crash.' Dallas could hear Clay pacing across the floor. 'Why didn't we face the facts and force Kyle to get help?'

'I blame myself. I never did understand Kyle.' Peter sounded bewildered.

'We can't change the past.' Clay sighed heavily. 'The important thing now is to do right by Nicky.' His voice changed. 'What have we here? Dallas's kitten must have got out of her room while she was sleeping.'

Dallas fled back to her room as quickly and quietly as her crutches allowed. Who said eavesdroppers never heard any good of themselves? Clay had been protecting her. Furthermore, there had been nothing between Clay and Alanna. She felt like shouting the news from the top of the Spanish Peaks.

Her happiness evaporated as quickly as it had come. If Alanna wasn't the obstacle between her and Clay, what was? Why was he so anxious to divorce her? Just because he doesn't love Alanna, it doesn't mean he has to fall in love with you, an inner voice chided. Dallas pounded her pillow. Darn it, why not? What was wrong with her? If Clay Dalton thought he could get rid of her just like that, he had another think coming.

She was ready for him by the time he brought up dinner. Nicky had been in and out all afternoon, and Dallas had read her a bedtime story, but she'd still had plenty of time to plan. Clay Dalton wasn't going to send her back to Virginia like a—a jacket he'd decided didn't suit him.

Clay set a tray in front of her and then cleared a spot from her bedside table. 'I thought I'd eat up here with you. I fed Nicky earlier, and the dining-room seemed awfully lonely.'

'You may as well get used to it,' Dallas said in an unfeeling voice. He needn't expect sympathy from her.

Clay shot a quick look at her. 'Ankle bothering you?'

'I'll live. I've been thinking about our divorce.' She took a bite out of her hamburger.

'And?' he asked, a wary look on his face.

'I think you've been most unfair. I sacrificed my home, my job, my friends—and all at your insistence. Do you really think that a casual "I'm sorry" makes up for all that?'

'No, I——'

'Good.' She bit a pickle in half. 'Because I'm going to give you a chance to show you're truly sorry. You can have your divorce. I'm taking Nicky, and,' she paused for effect, 'I want half the ranch.'

'Half the...!' Clay choked on the words. 'You're joking.'

'I'm perfectly serious. This marriage has been merely a minor inconvenience for you. Maybe if I make it more painful, the next time you have some hare-brained scheme, you'll think it through before charging full speed ahead, damn the torpedoes.'

'I don't know what kind of crazy trick you think you're pulling here, but you're not going to get away with it.'

'Crazy trick? You can accuse me of pulling a crazy trick? Who was the one who came up with the dumb idea of getting married in the first place?' Dallas asked.

'I admitted it was an asinine——'

'To call it asinine is to give it too much credit!' Dallas was yelling as loud as he was. She took a deep breath. 'You're going to wake up Nicky.'

'Yes, Nicky. You wouldn't want to forget her,' he jeered. 'After all, she's your excuse for being here. When did you decide that you were on to a good thing and that you might be able to get your greedy little hands on what's mine?'

'You're the one who called it "our place".'

'Only because we're married. Once we're divorced, dear wife, you won't own so much as the bed you're sleeping in.'

'Wrong,' Dallas said sweetly. 'This bed came from my family.' The rage boiling across the room gave her an immense feeling of satisfaction. 'Since you seem to feel so strongly about not sharing the ranch, perhaps we can bargain.'

'And how much is that going to cost me?' Clay asked grimly.

'The house.'

'If you think I'm going to let you sell this house that's been in my family since it was built——'

'Who said anything about selling? I intend to live here.'

'The hell you are. If you think——'

'Nicky and I have to live somewhere. For some inexplicable reason she's crazy about you and it would break her heart if I separated the two of you. She likes it here, and I don't want to move her. Then there's your father to consider. Nicky is his only grandchild and, based on the prospects, all he's likely to have.' Clay scowled at her, and she shifted on the bed, hoping her injury was enough to save her from being strangled. 'I considered buying a house in town, and then I decided, why should I when you have this perfectly good place here?'

'Where am I going to live?'

'You can live in town.'

'That might make running the ranch a little inconvenient.'

'Then live in the barn. And take that stupid cow downstairs with you.' This wasn't going at all how she'd planned. First Clay was supposed to be properly abject and then he was supposed to beg her to stay. He wasn't supposed to logically argue. The fact that he was proved he cared nothing for her.

Clay took a few steps around the room and then leaned one elbow on top of her chest of drawers. 'I thought you hated it out here.' His voice was deceptively mild, his face hidden in the shadows beyond the pool of light from her bedside lamp.

Dallas leaned back against her pillows, exhausted. Clay was determined that she leave. 'You thought wrong,' she said dully. 'Besides, Nicky belongs here.'

'And you'd sacrifice so she could stay?'

'It's no sacrifice. I like it here.' Her fingers prowled restlessly over the covers. 'I think I'm needed at the school. I like the people I've met. I know you don't think I fit in, but I'm happy here.' The silence that followed her declaration seemed to vibrate with tension.

Clay had moved to the window and was staring out into the dark night. 'You say that I owe you and that you want half the ranch. Fine. We'll split everything half and half. My way. To begin with, the house. It's too damned big for either one of us to live here alone. We'll split it down the middle.'

His dispassionate voice bewildered her as much as his words. 'Down the middle... I don't understand. You mean that you'll live in one half of the house and I'll live in the other?'

'I mean you get half of each room and I get half. Including the bedrooms.'

'The bedrooms...' Dallas repeated in confusion.

'And,' he continued relentlessly, 'the division includes my bed. Half is yours and half is mine.' He turned and glared at her. 'When I wake up in the morning I want to see your head on the next pillow. I'm sick and tired of separate bedrooms.'

'Now wait a minute!' Dallas sat up and glared back, refusing to acknowledge a faint tinge of hope. 'I'm not the one who sneaks out every night like some thief.'

'What did you expect me to do? I knew Nicky was in the habit of running in and crawling in with you in the morning. I figured you'd explain things to her and then I could stay. Or you would move into my bedroom. But you never did. At the hotel, when you came to my room you made it perfectly clear that sleeping with me was along the lines of a service station stop. Drop in, get what you wanted, and take off.'

'Of all the disgusting——' Her voice came to an abrupt halt. 'Is that why you were so mad the next day? I thought you didn't want me to stay? You always left me . . . I thought . . .'

'You thought what?'

'That you were sorry I wasn't Alanna.'

'Alanna!' he exploded. 'She's the last woman on earth I would have wanted to sleep with.' Clay moved to the side of the bed, a frown on his face. 'Where did you get that dumb idea?'

Dallas picked at the covers, unable to meet his eyes. 'Things people said. Your reluctance to talk about her. My—my nightgown. You knew she had one like it.'

He heaved a heavy sigh. 'I should have known that, even in her diary, Alanna wouldn't tell the truth.'

Dallas looked down at the abandoned tray sitting on her lap. 'I only read part of the diary,' she confessed. 'Alanna wrote about her affair with Terry.' She ignored Clay's indrawn breath. 'She called him D.P. I-I thought she was talking about you. Last night at the cabin I realised the truth.'

The crooked smile on Clay's face didn't extend to his eyes. 'What a nice notion of my morals you have. Believing that I would sleep with my brother's wife. You must think I'm perfectly capable of any perfidy.'

'I didn't want to believe it,' she cried, 'but you kept making all those cryptic remarks. And then . . . the nightgown . . .' she finished miserably.

'The nightgown. Yes, I'd seen Alanna in hers. She was wearing it when Kyle found her in my arms. Why the horror?' he lashed out as she recoiled. 'I told you about that before.'

'I'd forgotten,' she half whispered.

'Then let me remind you. The night Kyle died he was drinking because his brother had betrayed him with his wife. I'm as guilty of his death as if I'd shot him.'

'No.' The torment in his eyes pierced her heart. 'I don't believe it. Even if you did love Alanna, you'd never be disloyal to your brother. Honour is too important to you. If Kyle found her in your arms, there must have been an innocent reason.'

'What could be innocent about it?'

Hearing the anguish in his voice, Dallas reached out to him. 'I don't know. I just know you'd never hurt Kyle.'

Clay took the tray from her lap before dropping heavily on the edge of the bed. 'Kyle didn't have your faith in me. He died believing that I had betrayed him.' Overcome by his memories, Clay seemed to have forgotten her presence. 'I tried to explain, but how do you tell a man his wife threw herself into your arms? He was my brother. Why didn't he trust me?'

Dallas felt Clay's pain and struggled to find words of comfort. She remembered what Vicky Gomez had said. 'I think Kyle spent most of his life searching for an identity. Because you've always known yours, he felt somehow inadequate around you. Because he felt you were the better man, he thought it natural that Alanna would prefer you.' She slipped her hand into his.

'They fought about it, and Kyle was drinking that night. Their accident——'

'Was not your fault,' she said quickly. 'You weren't with them. You didn't know that he was drinking. You're not responsible for what Kyle thought or how he reacted.' Clay, she wanted to cry, he was weak, can't you see that? Instead she said, 'Alanna wasn't perfect, I understand that now. She had her demons to slay. More than anything in the world, Alanna feared being unloved. She always wanted to come first with everyone.'

'I know. Even at her wedding Alanna was jealous that I preferred you. She tried to tell me that it wasn't fair of me to drag you all over Washington DC to look at mouldy old buildings.'

Dallas blinked back tears. 'Poor Alanna. Driven to an affair with Terry, then falling in love with him so that she had to use you as a red herring to protect him when Kyle began to suspect her unfaithfulness. I know what she did was reprehensible, but she was always so terrified of being abandoned. The discovery that Kyle was having an affair...' Dallas correctly interpreted Clay's convulsive movement. 'It was in her diary, but I already knew from something Mercedes said. Alanna started the affair with Terry to prove to Kyle that she was worth loving. Then she was afraid of losing Nicky. She must have felt her whole life was being threatened by Mercedes.'

'About Mercedes. Our engagement just sort of happened. I was more relieved than heartbroken when she changed her mind.' Clay had discovered her hand in his and he was tracing the lines of her palm. 'You haven't said whether you'll accept my conditions of the divorce settlement.'

She closed her eyes to block out the gleam in his. 'It would be an awfully weird divorce.'

Clay laughed softly. 'We've had an awfully weird marriage.'

Disappointment stung her. Nothing had changed. Clay still wanted her to care for Nicky and warm his bed. Nothing more. 'And if I refuse your conditions?'

'I'll refuse to give you a divorce.' He swung his long legs up on the bed beside her.

'But you're the one who wanted the divorce.'

'It seemed the least I could do for you. You accused me of dragging you out here. Since then, you've fallen off horses, trucks, ladders, you've been lonely, tangled with rustlers, got lost . . .' He slipped his arm behind her shoulders. 'How was I supposed to know that's your idea of a good time?'

'Are you saying you don't really want a divorce?' Dallas asked carefully.

'Are you kidding? Dad, Sara, Jim, the school, the whole neighbourhood would rise up in revolt if I divorced you.'

'I see.' Her voice caught on a sob.

'That's more than I did for a long time.' There were wry undertones to his voice. He ran his fingers up and down her arm. 'Only a fool would propose marriage to a woman just to have someone to take care of his niece. You seemed the perfect choice. I remembered you as a sweet kid and I knew you loved Nicky. And marrying you took away the threat of your winning custody. Two birds with one stone.' His laugh was derisive. 'I was such a fool, I never considered beyond the court hearing.' He tilted her chin up with his finger. 'I never considered what would happen when a honey-blonde witch used her charms on me. The first time you fell off Molly and lay there on the ground joking about it, I felt as if a bolt of lightning had struck me.'

The tender light in his eyes took her breath away. . 'You—you said that love couldn't be forced, that you could never love me. You were always snarling at me.'

'I never said I couldn't love you. I thought you couldn't love me, and I didn't want you to feel guilty because of it.' He smoothed his thumb over her trembling mouth. 'Why do you think I snarled at you? Because I'd fallen crazy in love with you, and you made it quite plain that you were only interested in

Nicky. Unrequited love is enough to make a saint snarl.'

'You're hardly a saint,' she said automatically, her head awhirl with Clay's admission. He loved her!

Before she could respond to that, he lifted her hand to his lips and began kissing her fingertips. 'I've made a decision,' he said between fingers. 'From now on, I'm taking a lesson from you. You fall down, you get up. You never give up. Well, I don't intend to give up either. Not until you say you love me.'

'And if I never do?' she teased, her heart buoyant.

'I'll just have to persuade you.' He lowered his head.

'Clay,' she shrieked, 'you can't make love to me now. I've spent the day lying in bed with my foot in a huge cast, my hair is a mess, I don't have on any make-up, and I'm wearing an old flannel nightgown.'

'OK.' He flattened the pillow behind her, slid lower on the bed, crossed his hands over his chest and closed his eyes.

'OK, what?' she asked suspiciously.

'I won't make love to you until your ankle is healed, you've been to the beauty parlour, gussied up your face and you're wearing a new nightgown. I'll even buy it.'

She slipped down beside him. 'A green one. With ruffles.'

'Nope. Gold to bring out the gold highlights in your eyes. And slinky.'

'All right. Gold,' Dallas said, sliding a hand across his chest. 'You're the boss.'

Clay laughed.

my VALENTINE 1992

Celebrate the most romantic day of the year with
MY VALENTINE 1992—a sexy new collection of four
romantic stories written by our famous Temptation
authors:

GINA WILKINS
KRISTINE ROLOFSON
JOANN ROSS
VICKI LEWIS THOMPSON

My Valentine 1992—an exquisite escape into a romantic
and sensuous world.

 Harlequin Books

VAL-92-R

HARLEQUIN
PROUDLY PRESENTS
A DAZZLING NEW CONCEPT IN ROMANCE FICTION

One small town—twelve terrific love stories

Welcome to Tyler, Wisconsin—a town full of people
you'll enjoy getting to know, memorable friends and
unforgettable lovers, and a long-buried secret that
lurks beneath its serene surface....

JOIN US FOR A YEAR IN THE LIFE OF TYLER

Each book set in Tyler is a self-contained love story;
together, the twelve novels stitch the fabric of a
community.

LOSE YOUR HEART TO TYLER!

The excitement begins in March 1992, with
WHIRLWIND, by Nancy Martin. When lively, brash
Liza Baron arrives home unexpectedly, she moves
into the old family lodge, where the silent and
mysterious Cliff Forrester has been living in seclusion
for years....

WATCH FOR ALL TWELVE BOOKS
OF THE TYLER SERIES
Available wherever Harlequin books are sold

Janet Dailey
Americana

A romantic tour of America through fifty favorite
Harlequin Presents novels, each one set in a different
state, and researched by Janet and her husband, Bill.
A journey of a lifetime in one cherished collection.

Don't miss the romantic stories set in these states:

Available wherever
Harlequin books are sold.

HARLEQUIN *Temptation*

Rebels & Rogues

All men are not created equal. Some are rough around the edges. Tough-minded but tenderhearted. Incredibly sexy. The tempting fulfillment of every woman's fantasy.

When it's time to fight for what they believe in, to win that special woman, our Rebels and Rogues are heroes at heart.

Matt: A hard man to forget . . . and an even harder man not to love.

THE HOOD by *Carin Rafferty*.
Temptation #381, February 1992.

Cameron: He came on a mission from light-years away . . . then a flesh-and-blood female changed everything.

THE OUTSIDER by *Barbara Delinsky*.
Temptation #385, March 1992.

At Temptation, 1992 is the Year of Rebels and Rogues. Look for twelve exciting stories, one each month, about bold and courageous men.

Don't miss upcoming books by your favorite authors, including Candace Schuler, JoAnn Ross and Janice Kaiser.

RR-2